SUMMER CAMP SECRET

SUMMER FLING
BOOK 2

KAIT NOLAN

TAKE THE LEAP PUBLISHING

1

hy didn't I go with the sticky boobs?

Aspen Fairchild shifted in her seat, trying desperately to get some relief from the strapless bra that had gone rogue and apparently popped an underwire. Said wire was currently poking the underside of her left breast as if it intended to hold her hostage until the end of the wedding ceremony. She didn't dare try to adjust anything. Not while the photographer was snapping away, capturing the processional only a few feet from her position on the front row. So, she pasted on a smile she hoped didn't look like a grimace and tried desperately to focus on the happy occasion.

And it was a happy occasion.

A dozen feet away, beneath a simple, white wooden archway festooned with chiffon and accented with clusters of flowers, strands of pearls and crystals that shimmered in the fading sunlight, stood her father, Walter, waiting for his bride. As Tricia reached the head of the simple driftwood aisle and took his hand, he beamed bright enough to rival the setting sun. The nerves and the joy made him look at least ten years younger than his fifty-one years. Aspen hadn't known he could still be that kind of happy. She sure as hell hadn't seen him look like this since before they'd lost her mother to an aggressive form of breast cancer ten years before.

There'd been such a fast turnaround from her mom's diagnosis, to being told it was terminal, to having to say goodbye. There'd been no long, lingering sickness. No wasting away. No chance to adjust. It had been fast and brutal. Mere weeks. Then she'd been gone. Gillian's death had absolutely leveled them both. Aspen and her father had spent the past decade propping each other up because life hadn't turned out the way they'd expected, and neither of them quite knew what to do in a world without her mother.

Then he'd met Tricia Rogers, a divorced mom of two who'd been cautiously getting back out there after her youngest had flown the nest for college. Given the distance between Cooper's Bend, in the mountains of north Georgia, and Savannah, where Tricia lived, Aspen had been skeptical. But they'd made it work, and here they were, eighteen months later, tying the knot in a beachside ceremony on Tybee Island in front of family and friends.

"Dearly beloved, we are gathered here today..."

As the vows began, Aspen was painfully aware of how empty the groom's side was. A handful of her father's friends had made the trek from home, but she was the only blood family he had left. Tricia's side was bursting with people. Her two kids, her mother, some siblings, cousins, and a multitude of friends that proved how integrated she was into her community. The disparity made it crystal clear how little was holding her father in Cooper's Bend. They hadn't discussed where he and Tricia would be living. Aspen hadn't been able to bring herself to ask, because neither alternative was comfortable. Either he sold the house and moved down to Savannah with his new wife, far away from Aspen, or he moved Tricia into the home he'd shared with Gillian and inevitably changed the rooms that had become calcified with memory. Both options hurt. But Aspen wouldn't say a word to dim this hard-won happiness for her father. He deserved this second chance at love, no matter what it meant for her.

"I now pronounce you husband and wife. You may kiss the bride!"

Walter bent Tricia back in a dip made all the more dramatic against the magnificent sunset sky. Aspen led the cheers and applause, even as the bra continued to molest her. First chance she got, she was slipping away to a bathroom to deal with the thing. Even if that meant stripping it off and shoving it into the trash. It had been a hot day that was leading into what would certainly be a warm night. Maybe no one would notice her girls gone wild in the halter dress.

But the opportunity kept eluding her. In the wake of the ceremony, she got pulled in for family photos with the happy couple. Guests swarmed for more photos before the light faded. Aspen thought for sure she'd have a chance to get away as they all walked en masse through the sun-warmed sand up the beach to the resort where the reception was being held. But the wedding planner snagged her to ask a question about the cake cutting. Then Heidi and Everett, her brand new step-siblings, insisted she needed to contribute to the playlist for the reception. And somehow, she found herself seated for the meal without ever being able to get a moment alone.

As the food was served, she crossed her arms and tried to surreptitiously readjust things. That only forced the bra into escape mode, inching down her torso. The whole thing made her think of her mom, who used to say, "Strapless bras are like very rude and forward men. They start at the top and quickly work their way down."

The memory made her want to snicker, as she had during the prom dress shopping trip when Gillian had shared that little gem.

Definitely should've gone with the sticky boobs. Though Aspen hadn't been sure that they'd stay stuck, given the humidity of south Georgia in July.

By the time they'd made it through the meal and into the speeches, the recalcitrant bra was barely covering her nipples. On the plus side, the tender spot that had been abused for the past couple of hours was getting a bit of a break. As soon as the attention was off the head table, she was saying to hell with it and dashing for the bathroom.

From his place at the center of the long table, her father rose and took the microphone. He looked so dashing in his tuxedo, his salt and pepper hair ruffled by the ocean breeze.

"My dear friends and family, I can't tell you how overjoyed I am that all of you could join us tonight to celebrate with Tricia and me here on beautiful Tybee Island. This is a second chance at love that neither of us expected, and we're so excited to start our new life together as husband and wife."

Despite the pang in her chest, Aspen clapped along with the rest of the guests as he lifted Tricia's hand to his lips.

"To that end, some of you may be surprised to learn that I'll be moving to Savannah to join Tricia."

Aspen's breath wooshed out as if he'd sucker punched her. That was it then. The answer she'd been afraid he'd choose. Two more goodbyes she wasn't prepared to make.

"But Cooper's Bend will always hold such special memories for me. It was where I raised my beautiful daughter, Aspen. As such, while I start this new chapter, I can't imagine a better person to inherit the house there than her."

Wait. What?

Walter turned to face her, the green eyes he'd passed onto her shining with emotion. "Which is why it brings me so much pride to announce that I'm passing the house onto you, for you to make your own memories there, and maybe raise a family of your own someday. Aspen, sweetheart, you are the light of my life, and I know you'll fill that house with joy and laughter for years to come."

"Dad..." Aspen could barely get the words out past the lump in her throat. Relief made her limbs shake as she pushed herself up from the chair and moved to hug him.

His arms closed around her, warm and firm. An anchor when she needed one the most. "It wouldn't have been right for it to go to anyone but you."

"Thank you." Her voice came out barely above a whisper, and she was deathly afraid her waterproof mascara was about to be put to the test.

They stood in a swaying hug for a long minute, lost in their private bittersweet moment. Then the DJ started up music and called for the first dance.

Walter stepped back. "You gonna dance with your old man after this?"

Aspen sniffed back the tears that wanted to fall. "Absolutely. Go on. Tricia's waiting."

He bussed her cheek, then took his wife's hand and led her onto the dance floor.

Aspen couldn't wait any longer. She made a break for it, weaving her way through the tables and inside the resort to the bathroom. Bypassing the little seating area for women to take a few minutes to rest, she locked herself into a stall. For a long moment, she stood, hands braced against the door as she wrestled with emotion.

He was giving her the house. It was an amazing gift on so many fronts. He was moving, but he wasn't taking the last of her mother away from her. Letting her make the choice about what and how to change things. Knowing she needed that connection for a while longer. Beyond all that, the house was paid for, free and clear. Being able to move back in and avoid the burden of rent would give her the financial freedom to do... well, she didn't know what, because she hadn't ever had that kind of flexibility. Maybe she'd finally think about stretching the wings that had been clipped by her mother's death.

And that's all stuff to think about later. Right now, it's time to burn this bra.

Reaching back, she released the clasp and wiggled the offending lingerie out of her dress. The moment her breasts were free, she heaved a sigh of relief. God, that felt good. Bras had to have been a torture device invented by men. She examined the edge and found that not only had the underwire poked through, it had straight up broken in two.

"Free nippies, it is." She slid a hand into the bodice of her dress and massaged the abused boob, hoping to relieve some of the ache. The tissue on the underside was swollen and irritated.

Damned bastard bra.

Except... no, this wasn't just an irritated spot. She dropped the bra to the floor and used both hands to palpitate the flesh. There was a decided lump deep in the tissue of her breast.

Terror struck like a viper, stealing the strength from her legs.

She had a lump in her breast.

Just like her mother.

She pressed a hand to her mouth to hold back the scream welling up in her chest.

No. No, no, no. This can't be happening.

They'd found Gillian's lump when she was forty.

Aspen was only twenty-eight.

The exterior door opened, and female laughter floated inside as other guests came in to check their makeup or use the facilities. The sound jolted her back to herself.

This was her father's wedding. He was out there, waiting to dance with her. To celebrate his new beginning. She wasn't about to say or do anything that would ruin his day. Not now. Not until she saw a doctor and had a diagnosis confirmed. There was absolutely nothing she could do about this before Monday morning.

Aspen took another few minutes to get herself under control. Then she trashed the bra and strode back out to the party to dance with her father, in case it was the last time she ever had a chance to do it.

FROM SOMEWHERE BENEATH the depths of the covers, Brooks Hennessy registered the pounding on his door. He was done dealing with all the things. The funeral had been endured. Condolences had been accepted. Casseroles had been frozen. All the aftermath crap had been dealt with. It was the off-season. He had no further professional obligations. The death certificate had arrived yesterday. He had every right to hole up in his house for another two months, until time for pre-season training.

The pounding came again, louder this time.

Brooks tugged the comforter up over his head. If he didn't respond, they would go away.

Even as the thought crossed his mind, he heard the sound of the door opening.

Dammit, he should never have given them spare keys to his place.

The murmur of low voices sounded as they moved through the house. He knew what they'd see. A riot of empty takeout containers and beer bottles, endless stacks of dirty dishes, and mountains of unopened mail. He hadn't been planning on company. If they had a problem with it, they could kiss his ass.

"Shit, dude." The shock in Colter Coughlin's tone had Brooks hunching his shoulders.

"Go away."

Grady Prichard, the third member of their trio, slapped a hand on Brooks's leg on top of the blanket. "Can't do that, man. We're here to make sure that you're doing the bare minimum to take care of yourself."

"I'm fine."

Brooks wasn't even in the same country as fine, but he wasn't about to admit that.

"Somehow, we don't believe you."

Brooks sensed them on either side of the foot of the bed seconds before the duvet was yanked off him. He sat up, glaring. "You're lucky I wasn't naked under here."

Grady rolled his eyes. "Nothing we haven't seen before in the locker room."

"Speaking of which, you need to go shower."

Brooks transferred his scowl to Colter. "Go away."

His buddy didn't blink. "Not gonna happen. At least, not until you've showered, and we've seen you eat something."

Knowing them well enough to ascertain the truth of this statement, Brooks swung his legs out of the bed and sat up. His whole body hurt. He hadn't been keeping up with the workouts that maintained his physique as a pro athlete. Not even the low-level ones that were his habit during the off season. What was the point? He wasn't even sure if he wanted to go back. So he felt about a hundred years old as he stood and moved toward his friends. Grady made a Vanna White gesture toward the open bathroom door. "Please enjoy. We'll help take care of the rest."

"Leave it," Brooks growled.

Colter slapped a hand on his shoulder and squeezed. "Just go shower, man. It'll make you feel a little more human."

Not having the energy to argue, Brooks stumbled into the bathroom to do as they ordered. As he stripped out of his T-shirt and basketball shorts, he had to admit he did smell like something that had been left to molder in the back of his locker over the course of a full season. Kind of like the lucky socks he'd worn during his AHL career before moving up to the pros. He stepped under the spray and let it beat down on his head and shoulders, loosening up muscles gone stiff with inactivity. He stayed in the bathroom longer than necessary, with a vague hope that his friends would have disappeared by the time he came out.

No such luck. When he stepped into his living room, dressed in clean sweatpants and a T-shirt, they'd done their best impression of Merry Maids. All the takeout containers and empty beer bottles had been cleared away. The low rumble of the dishwasher told him they'd dealt with the dishes as well.

Colter eyed him from head to toe. "Well now, you look a little bit more like someone who's part of the land of the living." The moment the words were out of his mouth, Colter winced. "Sorry. But do you feel better?"

"Set the bar lower, man." Brooks's gaze slid to the counter, where he spied a large pizza box. "Is that pizza from Tremoni's?" He didn't want to be interested, but the scent of tomatoes and garlic and grease had his stomach growling.

When was the last time he'd eaten?

"An extra-large pie, just for you." Grady nudged over a plate. "Eat."

Brooks recognized an order when he heard one, but he didn't have enough energy to ignore it in the name of being contrary. He opened the box and lifted out a slice covered in pepperoni, peppers, onions, and mushrooms. This would be the closest he'd come to a vegetable in at least a week. He bit in, closing his eyes as the spicy sauce and melted cheese hit his tongue.

"He is responding to normal stimuli. This is improvement," Colter declared.

Brooks just fixed a flat gaze on his friend. He finished the first slice of pizza, washing it down with filtered water from the fridge. The food did help a little. "Thanks."

As he reached for another slice, his friends exchanged a look. "Do I look that bad?"

This time it was Grady who grabbed his shoulder. "You really don't want us to answer that. But you do look better since the shower. Even if your beard is making you look like a homeless Viking."

Fresh irritation prickled. "You've done your wellness check, seen that I've showered and eaten. You're free to go anytime."

"That's not what friends do, Hennessy. We want to be here for you."

Colter nodded. "Yeah, you've done the hermit routine long enough. It's time you start getting out in the world again."

"If either of you think that I have any intention of going down to Denver in search of a puck bunny at one of our usual haunts, you are sorely mistaken." The last thing Brooks wanted to do was go out in public and risk being recognized. He was the reason his team had been kicked out of the playoffs. It was possible that the commentators had moved on to something else by now, but he had no interest in putting that theory to the test.

Colter looked to Grady. The Canadian had no poker-face to speak of, and Brooks could easily see the concern underlying his attempt at discretion.

"What is it?"

"We're just here to check on you," Colter insisted.

But Brooks wasn't reassured. A little frisson of unease trickled down his spine. "What?"

Grady sighed. "We overheard Maxwell talking."

Damien Maxwell was the general manager for their team. If they'd overheard something he was saying, the only thing that would be of any interest would be about Brooks's fate on the team. "What did he say?"

"He's looking to trade you. "

Brooks waited for the emotional sucker punch to hit. This was his pro-hockey career at stake. The thing he'd devoted his entire adult life to. The reason his mother hadn't felt as if she could tell him that she was sick.

But the blow never landed. He lifted his shoulder in a shrug. "And?"

"We just thought you'd want to know." Colter didn't seem to have any idea what to do with his lack of reaction. Another worried glance passed between his friends.

To prove he wasn't bothered, Brooks picked up another slice of pizza. "It's to be expected after I blew the playoffs." In truth, he should never have gotten back on the ice after his mother's death. His heart hadn't been in it. But his team had been counting on him. And he'd screwed the pooch in a big way. Maxwell was well within his rights and his duty to the team in discussing trades with other teams.

"Do you know who he's negotiating with?"

"No. Yanovich ran us off before we could hear more."

Brooks shrugged again. "It doesn't matter. If he's looking to trade me, I'll get traded. I'll either go, or I'll retire."

Colter straightened. "Shit, dude. Would you really retire?"

Grady frowned so hard a line formed between his dark brows. "Yeah. I know you're in a bad way right now, but this is your career."

The career Brooks was no longer certain he wanted.

He wasn't angry with Maxwell. This was the nature of pro hockey. He'd known that when he signed contracts in the beginning nearly a decade ago. If he expected to feel something at the prospect of leaving Colorado, he was mistaken. All he felt was numb.

"What am I supposed to do about it?"

If his friends were offended that he wasn't making an effort to prove that he wanted to stay, or that he valued their friendship, they didn't show it. Instead, Grady braced his elbows on the counter. "We expect you to take care of yourself. Above the team, above us, we want to know that you're okay."

The idea of it was laughable. Not the thought that his friends cared—he certainly appreciated that, no matter how much he was growling at them—but the idea that he would ever be okay again in a world without his mother. A world where he hadn't been able to say goodbye.

"That's a tall order, man."

"We know. That's why we think it would do you good to get out of town for a bit. Take a little vacation."

"A vacation? You think I want to go visit a beach or some shit right now?"

Colter spoke up. "Not a beach. We were thinking the mountains. The middle of the woods. Something to suit your current grizzly bear personality." He softened the teasing with a little bit of a smile.

"The middle of the woods might not be so terrible," he conceded. He'd be far away from reporters and the not-so-well-meaning public who thought his grief was for their consumption.

"Good." Grady straightened with a nod. "We've already booked you a cabin in the Berkshires."

Brooks blinked. "You did what now?"

"We booked you a week-long stay at a grown-up summer camp on the other side of the country. You've been away from New York for long enough that you shouldn't be as easily recognizable over there as you are here. It should give you the privacy you want with the amenities of a resort. Let someone else see to the laundry and the cleaning and the food so you don't have to."

"It's called Camp Firefly Falls," Colter added. "Apparently it used to be a sleep-away camp for kids a long time ago, but some former campers bought it and turned it into a resort a few years ago."

Brooks was still staring. "You're sending me to summer camp?"

"You need a break. An all-inclusive resort somewhere tropical is not your jam, so this seemed like the next best option." Grady put an envelope on the counter. "All the information about it is in here. The only thing you've gotta do is book a flight to get to that side of the country. Your reservation starts end of next week."

"You expect me to just up and drop everything to fly across the country to go to summer camp?"

Grady arched a challenging brow. "Drop what, exactly?" He gave a pointed look around the house. "You're entitled to your grief, man. But we're not gonna let you wallow in it and drown. Take the trip. Think about something other than hockey for a bit. Maybe you'll have a clearer head when you come back."

He considered their offer. He wasn't exactly excited about going anywhere, but he recognized the kindness in the gesture. And maybe they were right. Maybe it would do him good to get out of town, away from everything that reminded him of his mom.

"Are you two coming with me?"

Colter grinned. "Only if you want us to."

Brooks dug up a faint semblance of his usual smile. "Now, why would I want to spend a week with your ugly mug?"

"That's what we thought." Grady pulled him in for a back-thumping hug. "I know everything about this is shitty. But you're gonna get through it."

Brooks gave in to the hug. "Thank you for caring. Both of you."

Colter pulled him in. "Anytime, brother. Have a good trip."

2

On Wednesday afternoon, Aspen strode down Cohutta Street in Cooper's Bend toward her best friend's coffee shop, The Sword and the Scone. Though the July sun was brutal, she felt none of the heat. She wasn't sure she'd ever feel warm again.

A bell jingled as she opened the door and stepped inside. As it was coming on two o'clock, the lunch rush was over. But there were still a handful of patrons scattered around the mismatched tables that lined either side of the long, narrow room that had been fashioned with beams and texturized walls to resemble the wattle and daub construction of old Europe. Numb, Aspen made her way toward the back, where Linnea

Barton moved behind the polished bar, working levers and buttons to produce the best lattes and espressos this side of Atlanta. Or so her reputation said. Aspen was a tea drinker. Linnea had her covered, too.

"Here you go, Mrs. Phillips. One Castle Cappuccino with cinnamon." Linnea slid the mug across the counter and glanced beyond her customer. "Aspen! You're back."

Somehow, Aspen managed to lift a hand in a little wave and muster some semblance of a smile when Mrs. Phillips, who'd been her Brownie Troop leader a lifetime ago, turned to greet her.

"How lovely to see you. How's your father? How was the wedding?"

Behind Mrs. Phillips, concern flitted across Linnea's face. So the smile hadn't been all that convincing. Not surprising. But Aspen understood the nature of the small town social contract. She was obligated to chat for a few minutes for the sake of politeness.

"It was lovely. He and Tricia are off for a two-week honeymoon around the Mediterranean."

"Do you want your usual?" Linnea asked.

"Yes, thanks."

While her friend went about preparing the

pomegranate green tea she preferred, Aspen shared some of the highlights from the wedding.

"I'm just so pleased for him to have found someone new. He hasn't been the same since your mama."

Aspen swallowed. "No ma'am."

"Will she be moving here?"

"Actually, no. Dad's moving down to Savannah to be with her. He's giving the house to me."

"Oh my goodness! That's quite the gift."

"It certainly is." Not that she'd been able to fully wrap her brain around that yet, given what else was going on right now.

"Your tea's ready, Aspen. Why don't you come on back to the kitchen and visit for a bit?" Linnea urged.

Grateful for the save, she turned to Mrs. Phillips. "It was good to see you. Give Mr. Phillips my best, won't you?"

"I sure will. And our congratulations to your daddy and his new bride."

"Of course." The smile she flashed felt like knives in her cheeks.

As soon as the older woman moved away, Aspen skirted the end of the bar.

"Hey, Adojah, could you watch the front for a few minutes?"

Cooper's Bend's favorite former librarian lifted her coffee in a toast. "I've got you, sugar. Go on back."

Aspen pushed through the swinging door into the back, away from any further prying eyes.

"Sit." Linnea emphasized the order by steering Aspen toward the four-top table tucked into one corner of the space.

She sank into a chair and reached for the cup Linnea offered as if it were a lifeline.

Hazel eyes sober, Linnea took the adjacent chair. "What did the doctor say?"

Aspen's fingers tightened around the mug. The ceramic was so hot, it all but scalded her palms. But she needed that sense of grounding. "They did a mammogram and an ultrasound. There's definitely something there."

"Oh, honey." Linnea closed a hand over her arm. "I know this is so scary. Did he say anything about what he thinks he could be?"

"He wasn't willing to speculate. Not without a biopsy." That was to be expected. She knew that.

"So, when is it scheduled?"

"It isn't yet." Because it was there, she sipped at the tea but didn't really taste it.

"What? Why not?"

"Because the surgeon has just left for a three-week vacation." Aspen couldn't hide the fury in her voice. "I very well probably have cancer, and he's more concerned with touring Australia and New Zealand. God forbid they find someone else who can do the surgery. Instead, I'm expected to wait and stew."

Linnea's fingers tightened in solidarity. "That's awful. And so stressful for you. But surely that means it isn't that bad if they're not concerned enough to find someone else who can do it sooner."

That was hardly a comfort.

"Given my family history, I could be dead by then. My mom barely had more than that." Tears burned in her eyes as all the fears she'd shoved down since she walked out of the doctor's office bubbled up to choke her.

Linnea scooted her chair closer and draped an arm around Aspen's shoulders. "Honey, I know you don't have a lot of reason to keep the faith in the medical establishment, but I feel certain that if they believed it was the same kind of aggressive cancer that took your mom, they wouldn't be waiting. They would absolutely find someone else. There are dozens... maybe hundreds of completely benign reasons for there to be a lump. It doesn't mean that it's the worst case scenario."

Objectively, Aspen knew that. But it was impossible not to go there with her mother's medical history. Aspen hadn't lived a life that made her believe in the less horrible scenarios. Hell, she hadn't really lived a life at all.

The tears spilled over. "This is so unfair. I've done everything humanly possible to reduce my risk. I don't drink. I don't smoke. I haven't had sugar in ten years. I avoid processed everything and am one step above vegetarian. I exercise. I get adequate sleep. And here we are. I'm twenty-eight, and I probably have cancer."

Linnea's fingers squeezed harder, and her voice took on a more forceful edge than usual. "You don't know that. I don't say that to dismiss your fears. But it's not good for you to jump immediately to the worst conclusion. You don't have enough information. Neither does your doctor. If you're that worried about it, go get a second opinion. There are a lot of doctors down in Atlanta. You can find somebody who would be willing to go ahead and move up the biopsy if you need answers quicker. There is absolutely nothing wrong with that if it would give you some peace of mind."

Aspen had considered that on the drive back to Cooper's Bend. She shook her head. "If it's the worst case scenario, that's not how I want to spend my last weeks."

"What are you saying?"

"My mom didn't have time for anything. There was all this stuff that she wanted to do that she put off to raise me. Things that she and Dad simply couldn't afford. Or they were waiting until retirement. When she was dying, the thing she kept begging me to do is not to wait to live. Not to put anything off. To take the risks. And what is it I've done? Exactly the opposite of all of that. I didn't go to my prom because I didn't know how much time she had left. I didn't go on my senior trip because she'd just died. I was so worried about Dad that I stayed close to home. I got my degree online. I've never been out of the country. I haven't taken any risks at all with my life. I haven't gone anywhere. I haven't done anything. I have lived the last ten years from a place of fear."

The idea that this was all she was gonna get? That scared the shit out of her.

With a speculative look, Linnea sat back in her chair. "So you want to spend the next few weeks doing something else?"

Aspen clutched the mug tighter. "Yes. I don't think I can take the chance that this is something simple and benign. Whether it's the aggressive form that took my mother, or if it's something that will kill me slower, I don't want to die without having lived."

"For the record, I refuse to believe you're dying. But either way, I think this is a good idea. With your business, you can be mobile. You can do some travel, see some things." Linnea crossed the kitchen to the little office and came back with a notepad and pen. "It's time for you to make a list. Everything you want to experience. Then we'll figure out how to make that happen."

"Oh my God! You're Brooks Hennessy!"

At the excited female voice at his elbow, Brooks just closed his eyes. It had been a mistake to come through New York. A mistake to think that he'd be able to enjoy some anonymity in a city he hadn't spent time in for years. And it had absolutely been a mistake to scrape off several layers of the Viking beard.

"I can't believe I ran into you. Aren't you supposed to be in Colorado, though? What brings a hockey star like you all the way to New York in the middle of summer? Vacationing a bit before preseason ramps up?"

He didn't respond. Didn't even glance over, lest she take that as encouragement. Not that it seemed she needed any.

Without invitation, she slid onto the stool next to his at the bar of his hotel. "Big fan. I know it's the off-season, so you can't be here for a game. Sure wish it was hockey season, though! I miss watching you out there on the ice. Shame about the playoffs."

Where the hell was the bartender? Couldn't she do Brooks a solid and come take this woman's order so he could slip away while she was occupied?

"As for me, I'm just in New York for a boring work conference. Yep, even us normal office drones keep grinding through the summer. But a girl's gotta make time for some fun too, you know? I'm Jenny, by the way."

Brooks ignored both the flirty tone and the hand she extended into his peripheral vision, and lifted his beer instead, wishing it was something harder.

Jenny remained undeterred. "Since we're both stuck in this random hotel anyway, we should hang out tonight! I'll show you some of the hot spots around here. Unless you had something... more relaxing in mind? No?" She nudged his shoulder with hers. "Come on, Brooks! Live a little. What happens in New York stays in New York, right?"

"That's so nice of you to offer to play tour guide for my fiancé and me." The southern drawl dripped with honey, but Brooks recognized the subtlety of blades underneath. "Sorry I'm late, baby. My Uber got stuck in traffic."

The newcomer slid neatly between him and Jenny, laying her left hand on his arm in a light but possessive touch. All their gazes dropped to the diamond on that hand.

Jenny's cheeks colored. "Oh, I..." she stammered. "Apologies. No harm meant. I didn't realize he was taken."

The blonde flashed a beauty queen smile that made her eyes sparkle. "Doesn't that just make you wish men got some kind of engagement jewelry, too? It would make things so much simpler."

"I... uh... yeah. Enjoy your time in New York." Jenny slipped off the stool and moved off down the bar.

The stranger boosted herself onto the vacated stool, turning her back to Jenny and dropping the proprietary hand. "Sorry for the interruption, but it looked like you could use a save."

Brooks blinked and braced himself for round two of unwanted come-ons. "Thank you."

Another smile, softer this time. A real one that reached those pretty green eyes. "Feel free to just ignore me while I sit here for a few more minutes to make sure she's left, or at least got the message that you'd rather be left alone."

She pivoted toward the bar and caught the eye of the bartender.

Brooks could have left it at that, but he found himself curious. "Where did you learn to do that?"

"Do what?"

He waited as she ordered a tonic and lime. "Cut her off at the knees in the most polite way possible."

She huffed a little laugh. "Sugar, I'm Southern. We're taught how to do that from the cradle."

"Judging by that accent, you're a long way from home. Do you live here in New York or are you visiting?" And why did he care? Two minutes ago, all he'd wanted was to be left alone.

The bartender delivered her drink, and she sipped. "Visiting. I'm in town taking in the sights and crossing off some bucket list items."

Despite the easy tone, something dark moved through those eyes and told him this was more than a whim. "Yeah? What all have you seen?"

"Ellis Island and the Statue of Liberty. Spent a day at the Met. Saw a Broadway show. Had a slice of pizza at Joe's, which was to die for. Tried some heavenly hand-pulled noodles at some hole in the wall I would never be able to find again."

"All excellent choices. What's left?"

"Definitely have to go to the top of the Empire State Building. Maybe dinner at Sardi's. I haven't decided yet."

"Is your actual fiancé helping you out with all that?"

"My what?" She glanced down at the ring. "Oh. I'm not engaged. This was my mother's ring. I usually wear it on my right hand. For the purposes of the story, it seemed prudent to swap it."

Brooks wanted to ignore the relief he felt at that news. But this woman was the first thing to spark his interest in months. Even if it was just a few minutes of pleasant, non-pushy conversation. "Well, I appreciate your quick thinking."

"What about you? Are you in town for business, or do you live here?" Her nose wrinkled a little in self-deprecation. "Is that a dumb thing to ask? Does anyone who lives in New York actually show up at a hotel bar?"

"The locals show up sometimes. At least they did years ago when I lived near the city. But, no,

I'm just passing through." He waited for her to press for more. To angle for an autograph or allude to the fact that she realized who he was. But she simply watched him as she continued to sip, as if he were just some random guy.

Huh.

On the TV behind the bar, some commentator on ESPN was interviewing the goalie of the team who'd gone on to win the Stanley Cup because of his once-in-a-lifetime save. Brooks jerked his head toward the screen. "You follow sports?"

The woman laughed and shook her head. "I don't follow any kind of sportsball."

"Sportsball?" he repeated.

"It seems a reasonable term to encompass most of them, given the big ones all have ball in the name." Her smile flashed again. "I guess our engagement was doomed from the start." She glanced around. "Just as well, as it seems your admirer has disappeared."

Draining her glass, she laid some cash on the bar. "It was nice talking to you. I hope the rest of your trip is quieter."

Shouldering her purse, she vacated the stool.

Brooks found himself pivoting toward her. "Would you like some company to see the rest of the sites on your list?"

When her brows nearly hit her hairline, he raised his hands. "If you'd rather not, I totally understand. But I've spent some time in New York before, and I could show you some things you might not see otherwise." Realizing how that might come off as suggestive, he rushed to add, "In a not creepy way."

She angled her head. "I thought you wanted to be alone."

"So did I." The words were out before he thought better of them.

Did he imagine that hint of a blush in her cheeks?

"Well, that depends."

"On?"

"Whether you know where I can find the best cheesecake in the city."

Brooks offered a hand. "I'm in your debt. I'm happy to take you on a tour of the top three."

After only a moment's hesitation, she placed her hand in his and smiled. "Then it's a good thing I'm starving."

3

"So, is the Empire State Building experience everything you hoped it would be?"

Aspen could hardly focus on the panoramic views of the city spread out below her because she was too aware of her companion. Brooks stood behind her, shielding her from being jostled by the crowds with his bigger bulk, bracketing her in with his hands braced against the railing. They weren't touching, but she could feel the magnetic presence of him just a few inches from her back. She'd been achingly aware of it all afternoon as he'd taken her to two different bakeries for truly exceptional cheesecake, before they'd made their way to the Empire State Building. He'd somehow magicked up VIP passes that enabled them to skip the miles long lines, though he'd fully denied it when pressed.

Sweet. Brooks was incredibly sweet. And fun and funny and charming. Aspen absolutely understood what had made the woman at the hotel throw herself at him. She was more than tempted to do the same. But propositioning a man she'd known for only a few hours was a much scarier thing than traveling on her own.

Still, she'd vowed to be braver for whatever time she had left, so she leaned back into him as she answered. "Well, yes, and no."

That big body relaxed against her, and one hand dropped from the wall to wrap around her waist, holding her to him in a loose embrace. Aspen sighed and closed her eyes, absorbing the sensation of body touching body, easily able to feel the impression of each finger where his palm wrapped around her ribcage.

"What missed the mark?" The warmth of his breath tickled her ear, and she fought back a shudder.

"The views are truly spectacular. But there's a part of me that's a little bit disappointed that the lobby doesn't look exactly like it did in *Sleepless in Seattle*. I've had that image in my head for most of my life."

His laughter rumbled against her back. "That's one of my mom's favorite movies." He paused, tensing. "Was."

It wasn't the first time she'd noted him slipping in and out of present and past tense. Aspen knew without asking that he'd recently lost his mother. She knew exactly what that was like. It gave them a kinship on top of the outrageous attraction, but he hadn't brought it up, and she understood well enough that he didn't want to talk about it. In all likelihood, this time here with her was a form of distraction. She was okay with that. Especially as he was serving in the same capacity for her.

"Mine and my mom's, too." Wanting to see his face, she turned in his arms, lightly gripping his waist so he didn't pull away. "My dad always promised to bring her up here some Valentine's Day, and they never got the chance."

Recognition and understanding flickered over his features. An unspoken acknowledgment of mutual loss. "Is that what this trip is about? Doing some of the things that your mom didn't get a chance to do?"

"Partly. I'm trying to do better about living my life without fear. That was a promise I made her that I've been very bad at keeping." It wasn't the casual flirtation they'd been bandying about all afternoon.

But he didn't pull back from her. "That's a pretty bold and important goal. I'm honored to be able to help out with that in whatever small way possible."

If Aspen hadn't been so intent on his face, she might have missed when his gaze dropped to her mouth. Was he thinking about kissing her? God, she wanted that. Wanted to see if this crazy attraction was more than one-sided. And wouldn't kissing a relative stranger at the top of the Empire State Building be an amazing story to add to her collection?

Before she could talk herself out of it, Aspen cupped his cheek, then rose to her toes and brushed her lips to his. They both sighed at the contact. Brooks' arm tightened around her, his free hand sliding into her hair so that those long, strong fingers cupped her nape. She might have initiated this, but he was the one in control here. Everywhere they touched, Aspen's body came alive, vibrating with need. Every cell, every atom, aligned itself toward him. And yet, for all the underlying heat sparking between them, his kiss felt comfortable and weirdly familiar. As if they'd come together like this hundreds of times before.

Would going to bed with him be the same?

Even as the thought flickered through her mind, Brooks eased back, grinning.

"I like the brave version of you a hell of a lot."

Heat bloomed in Aspen's cheeks. "Me, too."

"Are you ready to go?"

For a moment, she only stared at him, wondering if he was fully on the same page about continuing this somewhere more private.

"We've still got one more cheesecake spot on the list."

Cheesecake. Right.

"As delicious as the first two rounds were, I'm not sure I need more cheesecake." After a decade without sugar, any more and she was likely to be sick. "Are there any other New York foodie institutions I need to try?"

He winked. "I've got you."

And wasn't that a heady promise? Though Aspen knew that wasn't what he'd meant. She let Brooks tow her through the crowd and back to the elevator, giving herself a silent talking to.

Ask him for what you want. He's clearly not indifferent to you.

But she didn't manage to give voice to her proposition by the time they got to the bottom of their very long elevator ride. Nor did she bring it up during a truly stupendous meal of dim sum in Chinatown. His engaging conversation distracted her during a twilight walk through Central Park, where her hand found its way into his as if it belonged there. But she thought of it again as they crossed the lobby of their hotel and stepped into one of the elevators. They pressed the respective buttons for their floors and the doors slid shut, leaving only the two of them.

These hours with Brooks had made Aspen realize exactly how lonely she'd been. Every single thing they'd done had been more fun because he was with her. She didn't know how long he was in New York or where he was from or where he was going. They hadn't spoken about any of that. Today had been purely about being in the present. And the present had brought this incredible man into her life.

Even if he wasn't meant to stay, surely she could manage to invite him into her bed?

"It's been a really great day." She flashed a shy smile up at him. "I'm glad you came with me."

"So am I."

They stared at each other. Aspen's heart kicked into high gear as she struggled to find the words. Maybe her wanting showed on her face because suddenly his mouth was on hers again, desperate, hungry. As if some switch had been flipped, every reservation fell away, and she opened for him, her hands fisting in his shirt. He backed her against the wall of the car, his hips pressing into hers in a way that left no doubt he was on board.

"Come up to my room." She gasped it against his mouth.

"Hell yes." The words were a delicious growl as his hands streaked down her back to cup her ass and lift.

Aspen wrapped her legs around his waist, delighted and aroused by how easily he handled the weight of her. She used the higher position to thread her own fingers into the shaggy strands of his blond hair and took his mouth again in another greedy kiss. When the bell dinged to indicate they'd come to a stop, they pulled apart only long enough to verify it was the right floor before Brooks was striding off the elevator.

"Which way?"

"Left. Room 1463."

He practically sprinted down the hall. Aspen laughed, the joy of the moment overflowing.

At her door, she fumbled out her keycard, slipping it into the lock with a shaking hand. The light turned green, and she opened it. Brooks surged inside, spinning as the door fell shut and pressing her against it, his hardness nestled against the softness between her thighs.

Her head dropped back against the door with a soft thunk. "Oh, God, yes."

His mouth found her throat, suckling on the tender flesh just above her collarbone. "I need you naked, Aspen."

"Likewise. But I think we have to leave the door to accomplish that."

His chuckle was low and rough as he spun them away and staggered further into the room to drop her onto the nearest bed with a bounce.

Aspen giggled and watched as he stripped his shirt up and off, tossing it onto the floor. At which point, she stopped laughing. "Holy hell, you're built."

She'd known he was fit. Had felt the hardness of him when he'd held her earlier. But she hadn't imagined the six-pack abs or those indentations below his waist that made her just a little dizzy.

Brooks grinned and held out his arms. "Like what you see?"

"I might have to pay tribute to all your hard work with my tongue."

His blue eyes went dark as he set one knee on the bed and bent over her. "Only if turnabout is fair play."

Aspen cupped his cheek, feeling the rasp of stubble against her palm as she tipped her mouth almost to his. "Let me be clear. I want you. I want your mouth and your hands on me. And I really, really want to ride you until we both scream."

With a little nip of her lower lip, he gripped the hem of her shirt. "As you wish."

THE FAINT SOUND of a car horn blaring snapped Brooks awake. He blinked groggily at the rim of sunlight showing around the edge of the hotel's blackout curtains. Definitely morning, and late at that if the dim noise of traffic was anything to go by. That was no surprise. There'd been very little sleeping last night, as the fresh aches in his body attested to. It was, to his mind, the very best kind of sore. Already hard again at the memory, and wondering if he could coax Aspen awake for a lazy round of morning sex and a massive room service breakfast, he rolled over.

The bed was empty.

Brooks sat up, looking toward the bathroom. But the door hung open and the lights were off. He was alone. In *her* room. Where the hell was she?

Stretching a hand out, he touched the sheets

on her side of the bed and found them cool. So she'd been up for a while. Maybe she'd gone after coffee or breakfast? A glance at the clock told him it was getting on toward ten. Caffeine was definitely climbing the priority ladder.

Switching on the bedside lamp, he dragged himself out of bed and spotted a note propped up in front of the TV. Unfolding the piece of hotel stationary, he read her looping scrawl.

Brooks,

I had some existing plans that couldn't change and had to leave this morning. Please know that this was not some effort to ghost you. Thank you for being part of my memories of the Big Apple and for an absolutely incredible night. I'll never forget it or you.

I got you a late checkout, so take your time.

Aspen

That was it. No last name. No phone number. No invitation to email her or ever contact her again.

Brooks let the paper drop to the floor along with his mood and scrubbed a hand over his face. How could she just be... gone? Apart from the fact that the sex had been amazing, she'd been the first thing that had made him want to live and be and do things again. He'd really thought they'd made a connection yesterday.

How long ago had she left? Could he catch up to her? Maybe she'd said something to the front desk about where she was headed when she'd arranged for that late checkout.

"No, dumbass, if she wanted more time with you, she'd have left you a means to contact her." His morning-rough voice sounded too loud to his own ears in the empty room.

Aspen hadn't signed the note with her phone number and an invitation to call her. They'd had an amazing one-night stand, and she didn't want more.

On a groan, Brooks flopped back onto the bed. He wanted to wallow and bury himself again. But that wasn't an option. He needed to get his shit together, get up to his own room, and clean up so he could make the drive to the Berkshires for this summer camp thing that Grady and Colter had signed him up for.

Maybe that would be better. Get away from the city where he'd just made a hell of a lot of good memories with a woman he'd never see again.

Damn it.

Not quite up to doing the walk of shame to his own room yet, he availed himself of the hotel toiletries and showered in hers, washing off the night. Somewhere in the midst of letting the hot water pound on his aching muscles, it occurred to him that maybe she could've programmed her number into his phone or done that airdrop thing for her contact. Buoyed by the thought, he ducked his head under the water to rinse the last of the shampoo and grabbed for a towel, hitching it around his hips and striding from the bathroom, still dripping.

The clothes that had been in a pile on the floor were neatly folded in the chair, his phone set on the table beside it. Brooks lunged for it, swiping open the screen and scrolling his contacts looking for her name. But it wasn't there. Because she hadn't somehow left it for him.

Under the renewed weight of disappointment, he dropped back onto the edge of the bed. This was really it. No more Aspen. No more honeyed Southern drawl. No more smile that warmed his cold insides.

He swiped off Do Not Disturb to check the drive time up to Camp Firefly Falls. His phone began to ding and vibrate like a chihuahua on speed as dozens of notifications and messages hit at once.

Dread curdled in his belly. Nothing good ever came from this many notifications. It usually meant some kind of PR nightmare, and he really did not want to deal with more of that. Maybe he could ignore it.

"Right. Because that always works so well."

Still, he could wait a little while. Finish drying off. Get dressed.

The phone rang in his hand. Colter.

That seemed safe enough. Maybe he was just checking in. Or maybe he had news about the trade. Hell, maybe the trade was what all this hoopla was about.

"Morning."

"Holy shit, dude."

"What?"

"Don't you 'What?' me. You've got some explaining to do."

Brooks stared at the phone for a second. "About what?"

"About this. I just texted you a link."

Toggling over to his messages, he found the thread with Colter and clicked. The browser opened to *Stick Side Scoop,* a well-known pro-hockey gossip blog. Right there on the front page was a photo of him and Aspen kissing at the top of the Empire State Building. Some enterprising soul had zoomed in to circle the engagement ring clearly visible on her left hand. The one she hadn't gotten around to swapping back.

The headline screamed "Hennessy's Hat Trick: Hockey, Heart, and Now a Fiancée?"

Someone up there had recognized him and capitalized on a private moment. Not only that, but they'd leapt to some big conclusions. Never mind that was the fiction Aspen had spun back at the bar. That had been of the moment. Not intended to go beyond that one rescue.

Heart thumping, he lifted the phone back to his ear. "It's just a gossip blog. I'm not engaged."

"That's sure as fuck not what everyone is saying. And I do mean *everyone*. This has gone mainstream."

"How mainstream?"

"Google yourself, and you'll see."

So he did. And found page after page of results speculating on who the mystery woman was. After just one day, the entire world thought he was really engaged.

"Well, shit."

4

Aspen jolted awake, disoriented for a moment by all the chattering people around her. Then an engine groaned, and the bus lurched again as it sped up from the switchback on its way up a mountain.

Right. The bus to the summer camp resort she'd booked in order to squeeze in as much fun as possible before her biopsy. The bus she'd given serious thought to missing before she slinked out like a thief in the wee hours this morning to catch it.

Was Brooks awake yet? Had he found her note? Surely by now he had.

What was he thinking? Was he disappointed to find her gone? Relieved not to have to face an awkward morning after? Fear of the latter had contributed to her decision to keep her original plans rather than risk being rejected if she asked him for more than the one night. If that flew in the face of the whole Being Braver principle she was following, well, she considered it a tactical retreat. Plus, she'd spent a pretty penny of her savings on this camp resort, and she couldn't see wasting it.

All around her people were talking and laughing. The whole thing reminded her a little bit of *The Parent Trap*, which was another of her mom's favorite movies.

As she blinked away the remnants of sleep, she realized that many of her fellow passengers kept looking at her. Self-conscious, she discreetly wiped at her mouth, wondering if she'd been drooling in her sleep.

"—can't wait to see what's changed since we were kids."

"I know, right? I *loved* Camp Firefly Falls back then. I'm so excited to be going back."

All around her, conversations echoed more of the same. A lot of the other folks on the bus had apparently been campers at Camp Firefly Falls back when it had been a normal sleep-away camp for kids. Maybe that was the source of the curious glances. She wasn't one of them.

Aspen firmly shoved down the vague sense of trepidation at that. Being on the outside was nothing new to her. But it made her miss Linnea. She wished desperately that her friend had been able to get away and come up here for this impulse trip. But she couldn't get away from the coffee shop that easily. Not without a lot more notice to arrange coverage.

Feeling a little lonely, she pulled out her phone to text Linnea.

> Aspen: I miss you. I'm on the bus to camp. I think we're nearly there.

She followed it up with a quick photo of the mountainside from out the bus window.

Linnea wrote back almost immediately.

> Linnea: I'm so excited for you! This is going to be a great trip. How was New York?

Aspen thought back to Brooks. *Life altering.* She began to type.

Aspen: New York was fantastic. Saw the sights. Ate lots of really great food.

Her fingers paused before adding "met a guy." That would make it sound like he'd continue to be in her life. Beyond all that, their time together felt like a secret just between the two of them. Something she wanted to hold close. Maybe because she hadn't yet processed the grief that he *wouldn't* be in her life beyond one fleeting day. He'd been utterly wonderful, and she'd have loved to stay in New York and spend more time with him.

Not that there'd been any guarantee that he'd have wanted to spend more time with her. Maybe he was a one-and-done kind of guy. How would she know? She just knew he'd given her the best sex of her life and a boatload of incredible memories. Aspen thought maybe her mom would be proud she'd taken life by the horns, as it were. She also would've been the first one to chastise Aspen for not getting his contact information or even his last name. That would have required waking him up and facing that prospectively awkward morning after.

She could've left her own number, and she'd considered it. But ultimately, it was better this way.

If she really did have cancer, the last thing he needed was to get involved with her. And yeah, okay, she could admit to herself that she couldn't quite take it if she'd left her number, and he never contacted her again. After how she'd left this morning without a word other than a note, he'd be well within his rights to be angry about being ghosted. Even though she'd expressly said in that letter that she wasn't ghosting him. Surely ghosting would involve not leaving any message at all?

No. Better to have that one perfect night stay perfect in her memory than to find out it hadn't meant as much to him.

So, Aspen sent the text without adding anything about Brooks.

A cheer went up around her as the bus took a wide turn onto a gravel drive beneath an arch reading Camp Firefly Falls.

Here at last.

She joined the happy chaos, spilling off the bus with everyone else and lugging her suitcase and backpack toward the pair of tables at the edge of the parking lot to get her cabin assignment. It took a while, but nobody seemed to mind. Aspen certainly wasn't in a hurry. The name of the game today was low key.

A ponytailed blonde flashed a broad smile when Aspen stepped up to the table. "Welcome to Camp Firefly Falls! I'm Heather Tully, one of the owners, and this is Stephanie Garcia. What's your name?"

"Aspen Fairchild."

Heather blinked, a flash of something that might have been recognition passing over her face. Which was ridiculous. Aspen didn't know this woman from Adam's house cat. They'd never met before, and certainly she had no reason to recognize Aspen's name. Heather exchanged a quick look with Stephanie, then consulted her list.

Maybe I imagined it.

Except, no. Stephanie was kind of staring at her with a kind of awe. What the hell was that about?

Heather frowned and checked something else. "There's been some confusion. You're listed over here in Cabin 12, but you should actually be in 27."

It made no difference to Aspen. A cabin was a cabin, right?

"I'm not fussy. So long as there's a bed and hot water."

The two women conferred in low tones before Heather finally announced firmly, "Definitely Cabin 27." She offered a key with another broad smile that had odd, *wink-wink, nudge-nudge* over-tones. "I hope you have a wonderful stay with us."

Too tired to parse out what any of this meant, Aspen took the key and offered map and hit the path toward her cabin. She'd dozed on the bus, but it hadn't been good sleep. After last night, she was exhausted. Maybe she'd settle in and have a nap before exploring the rest of the campus. After all, no one was waiting on her. This trip was en-tirely about what she wanted.

She passed the main lodge and followed the directions she'd been given, finding Cabin 27 easily enough. Like its neighbors, there were three steps up to a little porch with Adirondack chairs for sitting and looking at the lake. She used the key to let herself inside.

Oh, this was lovely. Definite shades of summer camp, but elevated. Rustic elegance. There was a king-size bed. Well, it seemed as if it was actually two twin beds pushed together and made up as one. Plenty of space for sleeping, which was far more than she'd been expecting. The cabin was air-conditioned and nicely appointed, with a mini fridge and microwave tucked into one corner, and a pair of desks built into the front, facing the lake. That would be handy if she decided to do any work on this trip. A little binder provided informa-

tion on all the amenities, including the wi-fi pass-
word. She'd investigate that later. First things first:
she wanted a shower. Then that nap.

Satisfied with her plan, she dumped her bag
on the bed, dug out her toiletries and stepped into
the bathroom.

BROOKS WAS STILL on the phone with his publicist
when he pulled into the parking lot at Camp
Firefly Falls.

"I really wish you'd gotten in touch with me
sooner." The note of rebuke in Rebekah's voice was
unmistakable. "I don't know how easy it's going to
be to correct the public's conception at this point."

He'd avoided this call for most of the day because, while his engagement wasn't real, at least
people were talking about something positive instead of making a public spectacle of his grief.
That part had been kind of nice—even if he hadn't
known what the hell to say to the handful of well-
wishers who'd congratulated him before he'd
made it out of the city. But he'd been forced to finally take Rebekah's call on the drive and give her
the truth about how all this had happened.

"Is it that terrible?"

She waited a beat to speak. "Is it terrible that you're fake engaged?"

"I mean, nobody knows who she is. They don't have her face or her name."

Rebekah tsked. "Oh, sweet summer child. They may not have her name... yet. But they will. They definitely have her face. As soon as that lip-lock photo surfaced, more people who were there started sharing their own pictures. You might not have been the focus of those shots, but you're in them, and so is your mystery girl."

Which meant, in theory, that eventually Aspen might hear about this. Even if she wasn't into "sportsball", as she put it, people who knew her would be. Would she think this had been his idea? Would she use it as a reason to contact him? Did he want her to?

Yeah. Yeah, he did. And what did that say about him?

When he said nothing, she continued. "I'll be in touch by the end of the day with a plan for how we're going to proceed."

"Great." He muttered it without enthusiasm, because whatever her plan was, it would involve him reverting to an object of pity. "Just don't make any statements or press releases without running them by me first."

"Understood. And do me a favor? Lay low, please."

Brooks promised he would, then hung up, folding his arms over the steering wheel with a sigh. Why could nothing be easy? Maybe it was good that he was up here in the middle of nowhere. Perhaps the news wouldn't have spread this far.

Wanting nothing more than to hole up, he grabbed his bag and went to the check-in table that had been set up at the edge of the parking lot. The low-level excitement of the two women attending it disabused him of the notion that he'd be flying entirely under the radar.

"We have your cabin ready, Mr. Hennessy." The blonde offered him a key and a map. "It's circled just there. I hope you and your... cabinmate enjoy yourselves."

Cabinmate?

He hadn't realized he'd be sharing his quarters. But this was meant to be a sort of summer camp kind of deal. Maybe that was part of the experience. Fine. It would be something else to distract him from thinking about Aspen.

With a short nod, he muttered, "Thanks."

Shouldering his bag, he checked out the directions and followed the path laid out on the page.

The camp was expansive and beautiful. The trail he followed led him around the curve of Lake Waawaatesi, which reflected the blue bowl of the sky like a mirror. Just the sight of that calm water had some of the knots unraveling. Maybe Grady and Colter were right. Maybe time out here in the woods would do him some good.

He found his cabin and stepped inside. The sound of the shower told him his roommate had already arrived. Then he noticed the bed. The one bed.

Well, that was a problem. Had they thought he was here actually with someone? Hell, he'd assumed his roommate would be a dude. Then again, maybe it was, and they were making a whole different set of assumptions.

Or maybe it was all a simple mistake.

It appeared the king-size bed was actually two twins pushed together. He'd just contact the front desk—Brooks assumed there was such a thing in the main lodge—and request new bedding. Just as he started to turn, the bathroom door opened and a cloud of steam spilled out. With it came a very not male, very naked-but-for-a-towel form.

"Um—"

At the sound of his voice, she screamed, clutching at the towel and pressing back against the wall in terror for three long seconds before her mouth dropped open. "What are you *doing here?*"

Brooks picked his own jaw up off the floor because during those three seconds, recognition had struck. "What are *you* doing here? Did you follow me?"

Aspen's face was utterly blank. "How could I have followed you? I left first thing this morning to catch the camp bus. Did you follow me?"

"No. My buddies booked me a session here to get away from shit at home."

They stood staring at each other in awkward silence for several long moments before Brooks finally blurted, "Why didn't you say goodbye?"

She dropped her gaze, a blush spreading from her cheeks down her creamy throat and lower to the chest he could still remember the taste of. "I've never done that before."

Brooks jerked his focus determinedly back to her face. "Ghosted somebody?"

Her head snapped up, eyes flashing. "I didn't ghost you. I left a note. I meant I've never had a one-night stand before. I didn't know the protocol, and I had to catch the bus." The brief flash of temper faded, and her eyes softened. "I truly am sorry. If it makes you feel any better, I've been kicking myself all day for not talking to you before I left."

To end things face to face, or because she wished they hadn't ended at all? If luck was on his side, he might just get the chance to find out. The desolation he'd felt since he'd woken to find her gone lifted at the prospect.

Mollified by the idea that she regretted walking away, Brooks tried to focus on their current situation. "Okay, so we both separately had travel plans to Camp Firefly Falls. How did you end up in my cabin?"

Aspen scooped a hand through her wet hair, nearly dislodging the towel in the process. "The camp people told me there was some confusion with my cabin and that I had been moved from my original one. I don't have any idea why. It must be some kind of administrative mix-up."

No. It was a lot more deliberate than that. Suddenly, the *wink-wink, nudge-nudge* of his exchange with the check-in staff made sense.

"I might know why."

"I'm all ears."

"Because we're engaged."

Aspen laughed. "I'm sorry, what?"

Brooks pulled out his phone and did a quick

Google search for his name, then handed over the resulting social media explosion, stepping back so he didn't give in to the overwhelming temptation to touch her again.

With every page of results and comments, her eyes got bigger and bigger. By the time she lifted her gaze to his, her eyes were jade saucers. "You're famous?"

At the gobsmacked look on her face, he nearly laughed. "I mean, kinda. I play hockey."

Her expression of utter bafflement was both adorable and confirmation that she really, really hadn't known who he was. Damn if he didn't like that. When was the last time anyone had been interested in him purely for him? Not since he'd taken the ice by storm nearly a decade before.

"I'm sorry for how this has bled over on you. Or will. They haven't figured out who you are. Yet. But they will. Because clearly the camp staff figured it out, and they're trying to help us out."

Her mouth opened and closed a few times. "Well, obviously that's not what I expected when I faked being your fiancée at the hotel bar."

Abruptly seeming to register her state of undress, she clutched the towel closer. "I should get dressed so we can sort out the cabin arrangements and what to do."

"Right, of course. But maybe…" Brooks trailed off, his mind going a hundred miles per hour.

"Maybe what?"

If Fate had delivered Aspen into his lap a second time, that had to mean something, right? His mom had been all about Fate and signs. She'd have been having kittens of excitement over this. He could practically hear her at his shoulder telling him not to waste this opportunity.

"Well, I have a proposal."

5

Aspen was achingly aware she was wrapped in a towel and nothing else. She had been aware of that fact from the moment she'd stepped out of the bathroom to find her cabin not empty. But that state of affairs had shifted from an acute sense of vulnerability to one of arousal at the recognition that the intruder was her incredible one-night stand. Or, she supposed, she was the intruder in his cabin if what he said was true. She wasn't entirely certain what was going on with that. But during the whole of their conversation, she'd been imagining dropping the towel and dragging him back to bed.

Any notion that she'd imagined or inflated last night in her head had disappeared at the sight of him in the broad light of day. Her skin tingled with awareness and remembered caresses. The man was an enthusiastic and generous lover, and she hadn't been able to stop thinking about him since she'd left him in her bed. Which meant she really needed to put some clothes on. Like... now.

But at his words, she stopped and took a firmer grip on the towel. "What kind of proposal?"

Brooks shoved both hands into his back pockets and rocked back on his heels. "As you saw, the 'news', such as it is, has already broken. Neither of us is going to get any peace at all if we go ahead and correct everybody's assumption about our engagement. Everyone's going to want to know the 'real' story or will make up their own version and ask us about that." He winced in a way that made it evident he'd had plenty of experience with that precise shade of intrusion. "The whole point of this vacation for me is rest and relaxation. I presume that there is at least some component of that for you, where you do not want to be fielding questions left and right from complete strangers."

Even the idea of that made her shudder. "The point of my trip isn't precisely rest and relaxation, but being in the public eye is definitely not on my agenda, either."

"So, we can just be cabinmates. Get new bedding and push the beds apart, and I'll otherwise leave you be if that's what you prefer—"

Disappointment lanced through her, sharper than she'd have expected considering she hadn't thought to see him again after this morning.

"But—"

Hope fountained up at that single syllable. Aspen desperately wanted to know what the 'but' was.

"The alternative is that we continue where we left off last night, which, frankly, is my preference. Because you are the first thing that has been good in my life since my mother died."

His words left her speechless. This wasn't the "Hey, the sex was really great. Let's keep going," surface kind of thing that she might have expected. But then, nothing between them had really been surface. That had been a huge part of the appeal of him. The rawness of the statement spoke to her. Because she remembered what it was to be where he was now—in the throes of recent grief he didn't know how to process or wade through.

When she didn't speak, he lifted his hands. "I realize that's a lot of pressure. That's not my intention at all. But you have this thing you're trying to do. Living more bravely. Experiencing more of life. I don't know... working on your bucket list, whatever. We can talk more about that later. Whatever it is, I can help you with it." He took a half step forward before stopping himself. "I think we can basically help each other and enjoy each other in the process."

Those big, clever hands fell to his side. "Of course, if you'd rather call the whole thing off, we can go talk to the front desk and get the cabin situation sorted and do our best to avoid each other for the week that we're here."

Because she could see that he needed the reassurance, she offered him a tentative smile. "I don't want to avoid you, Brooks." Scooping a hand through her hair, she took a firmer grip on the towel and began to pace. "I need to think."

Of course, she wanted to say yes. Every cell of her body was proclaiming it loud and clear. But she needed to make sure that it wasn't for the wrong reasons.

He had an excellent point that she'd get asked about him at every turn if they did end up correcting people's assumptions. Probably that was going to happen anyway, when all this was over. But it definitely would put a damper on her time here at the resort. She didn't want to have to explain herself to people, and she didn't want his vacation ruined either. He needed this time. She understood that.

The goal of this trip for her was to get out of her comfort zone and live, in case this was the only chance she got. Doing all that with him by her side would be infinitely more enjoyable. As would the multitude of orgasms she'd be racking up, which were incredibly hard to argue with.

Even standing here now, she wanted him again. Still. Or maybe she hadn't stopped wanting him from the moment her lips had touched his. She simply hadn't expected to have the opportunity to pursue that kind of pleasure again.

And here he was, offering to help her with whatever was on her Life List. Not that he knew or understood her motives behind all that. Nor would she tell him. He was still wounded from the loss of his mother. No way would Aspen put a damper on things by bringing up the fact that she was doing all this because she might be dying. They hadn't known each other long, but she understood that it would hurt him, and that was the last thing she wanted to do.

Aspen thought of her mom. She'd have been absolutely delighted by how all of this had happened. She'd have considered the whole thing a grand joke of the best sort. A kick in the ass from the Universe for her fearful daughter who otherwise couldn't get out of her own way.

If she said no and went back to Georgia in a week or two and found out that she wouldn't get a lot more tomorrows or any sort of a future, would she regret not taking him up on his offer? If this was the only living she got the chance to do, then a flaming hot affair with a gorgeous, sexy, charming pro hockey player would be a pretty great way to go out. How many people could say they got to do that? And maybe, if they spent more time together, she could do something to help ease his transition through the grief, as someone who'd been there.

Aspen closed the distance between them, still clutching the towel, and extended her free hand. "You have a deal."

His eyes lit as his big hand closed around hers, warm and sure. There was no question this was what he'd wanted. That he was excited and relieved.

Aspen felt that tangle of emotion herself, as she angled her head to look up into the intensity of her gaze. "Fairchild."

"What?"

"My name. It's Aspen Fairchild. If we're going to be engaged this week, it seems a thing you should know."

He shocked her by lifting the hand he held to his lips, brushing the barest of kisses across her knuckles. "It's nice to meet you properly, Aspen Fairchild."

She didn't fight the frisson of desire this time. Aspen had a feeling that this week, she wouldn't be fighting much of anything at all.

"LET ME GET THIS STRAIGHT. You want to continue this fake engagement, and she's agreed to this?"

"Yes, that is the plan." Brooks could tell by the lengthy hesitation before Rebekah responded that she thought this was a terrible, terrible idea.

But what she said next wasn't the caution he expected from her. "You do know that the longer this goes on, the more real it's going to feel, right?"

He blinked. What did that matter? Both he and Aspen were well aware of what the terms were going into it. He just wanted to make sure his publicist was on board. "I know exactly what this is. In the meantime, the party line is 'no comment' or, at best, 'thank you' for any congratulations."

Rebekah blew out a long breath. "Understood. But Brooks—"

He didn't want a lecture. He just wanted to

enjoy the miracle of getting this extra time with Aspen. "I've gotta go. I'll be in touch after my vacation." Before she could say anything else, he ended the call.

The afternoon had been exactly what he'd needed. They'd cuddled up and had a lengthy nap —only a nap—which had been surprisingly wonderful. Now they were about to go have dinner at the five-star restaurant that was part of the resort.

The bathroom door opened behind him, and Aspen stepped out again, looking like a million bucks in a little sundress that flirted with her knees and showed an expanse of tan leg. A pair of low-heeled sandals showed off toes painted a vibrant pink. Had she done that somehow while he was waiting? He hadn't noticed her toes last night. Her pale blonde hair was loose around her shoulders, and tiny silver hoops winked in her ears. Two pair. Why was that unaccountably sexy?

"Ready?"

She flashed the engagement ring she'd moved back to her left hand to hold up their cover. "All set."

Brooks extended his hand for hers. "My lady."

With a shy little smile, her fingers slipped into his.

This felt different from the flirtation they'd

had in New York. Like they were actually taking their time to sort of... date. Which wasn't a thing he'd have said he wanted, had anyone asked him before this moment. But right now, it felt pretty great.

They walked from their cabin down to the path that wound alongside the lake. Other campers were out and about, headed to or from various activities. Canoes and paddleboats broke the stillness of the water and laughter floated on the faint breeze. From the little book he'd perused, he knew there'd be a campfire cookout for those seeking a more casual dining experience for the night. And there was some sort of an opening session dance later, followed by campfire s'mores, which, according to the brochure, were not to be missed. He couldn't remember the last time he'd had a s'more.

The restaurant was located inside the main lodge. A low murmur of voices told him they weren't the only ones with this as their dinner destination. A half-dozen people milled around in the lobby near the hostess stand.

"Table for two, please."

The hostess checked her book. "It's going to be a few minutes. Would you like to wait here or at the bar?"

A glance in the direction of the latter told him there were a lot more people to contend with. "Here's fine."

"I have you down, sir."

"You don't need my name?"

Her lips curved. "No, sir."

"Okay, then." He nudged Aspen to the side, so they'd be out of the way.

She tucked herself close to his side. "Does that happen often? Being recognized?"

"More so back home than anywhere else. But also in New York. I spent several years in the area at the start of my career. I'm not sure exactly what the deal is here, except that maybe my teammates who booked this place asked for some kind of VIP treatment. Or maybe one of the owners is a hockey fan." It didn't matter to him, so long as people stayed respectful. Preferably at a distance.

"Oh my God. You're Brooks Hennessy!"

You know better than to challenge the Universe like that.

Bracing himself, Brooks turned to face the newcomer, a nineteen or twenty-something kid with veritable stars in his eyes. "Guilty as charged."

"Man! I'm a big fan. Could I possibly get your autograph?"

Fan service was part of the gig, so he tamped down any annoyance. "Sure."

The kid patted his pockets and came up with a rewards card from a frozen yogurt place. The hostess offered a pen. Brooks signed the card and handed it over.

The boy looked at him as if he'd hung the moon. "Thank you!"

"No problem." Brooks turned back to Aspen.

"And I just wanted to say I'm really sorry about your mom."

The condolences blindsided him, even though this had happened a lot in the weeks after her death. Aspen curled her arm through his and squeezed, pressing close, grounding him in the moment, and he was so damned grateful not to be alone in all of this.

"Thank you." It was barely a mumble.

"Could I get a selfie?"

Brooks could only stare at the guy's hopeful expression, his gut in far too many knots of fresh grief.

A soft hand curled around his arm. "You're so sweet, but my fiancé and I are really just here for a nice meal and some downtime. You understand."

Brooks covered that hand with his, squeezing

in mute gratitude as Aspen came to his rescue yet again.

The kid looked to her, his cheeks coloring. "Oh, of course. I'm sorry. Um, congratulations! Thank you for the autograph."

Thankfully, the hostess returned to take them to their table, saving him from further conversation.

Once seated in a reasonably private little alcove by the unlit fireplace, their server materialized to take their drink orders.

"Bourbon on the rocks." Just one, to dull this stab of fresh pain.

"Whatever the house red is, please."

Once the server disappeared again, Aspen leaned toward him. "It has to be really hard."

"What?"

"The fact that your grief has been very public."

His gaze flashed to hers.

"I didn't look anything up. And I'm not going to, because whatever is out there for public consumption probably isn't the truth. So I don't know anything about this more than what I've observed. But if random strangers are coming up and asking for your autograph and making these remarks, it's obviously out there, and that's got to be hard."

A huge part of his attraction to this woman was

the fact that she didn't really know who he was as a public figure. That, even now, she was trying to get to know him for him was a really big deal. So he didn't blow off the comment. "Yeah. In fact, it sucks. The details of her death aren't out there, but that doesn't stop people from commenting."

He waited for her to ask what had happened. To pry for more information. But she didn't do any of that. She simply sat, waiting quietly, giving him the space to tell her whatever he wanted. Even if it was nothing at all.

So he found himself speaking. "It was... an illness. She didn't tell me she was sick. I don't even know how long she was sick. So when she died, it was completely unexpected. And it fucked with my head."

Her hand covered his on the table. "Of course it did. That's awful."

Their server returned with drinks and to take their orders. Neither of them had even looked at the menu.

"Steak. Medium rare. Loaded potato. Steamed veggies." That seemed a safe enough bet.

"The special for me. Thanks, sugar."

With a quick nod, the server disappeared again.

Brooks could have used the interruption to

change the subject, but he didn't. "I shouldn't have been playing right after she died. I jacked up my team's chances in the playoffs. Which is the other reason that I'm big in the news right now."

She picked up her wine and sipped. "Is that why you're up here? Escaping?"

"Somewhat. I caved up the last few weeks since the funeral. I took care of all the things. It's off-season right now for us." Remembering she knew nothing of "sportsball," he explained, "The normal hockey season starts in October, and the playoffs usually begin around mid-April. We were kicked out of the running in mid-May. I've basically got the summer to get my shit together and decide what I want to do before pre-season training starts."

"What do you mean?"

He could've talked about the likelihood of being traded. Of all the professional implications. But instead, he talked about where he'd started. "I put on my first pair of skates when I was five. My mom used to take me as soon as the ice was thick enough."

"Like... outside?"

"That is the norm where I'm from in Michigan."

Aspen pointed to herself. "Georgia, remember?

There's nothing normal about frozen lakes to us. Did you have a Hans?"

"A what?"

"A Hans." She flashed a smile. "You'll have to forgive me. The sum total of my knowledge about hockey comes from Disney's *The Mighty Ducks*, and if I remember correctly, the old dude who supported Gordon was Hans."

Impossibly, Brooks laughed. How could she do that? Give him laughter in the middle of the grief? "No. Just my mom. She was the one who first put a stick in my hands. I declared when I was six that I wanted to go pro. And instead of telling me 'That's nice, dear, now go get a real job,' Mom encouraged me. She did everything she could to support me. Worked extra jobs to cover the costs of equipment and fees. She was my number one biggest fan. She came to all of my games, going from peewee on up to the pros. When I landed a slot in the AHL— that's more or less minor league hockey—she could not possibly have been prouder. She was how I got from that skinny little six-year-old kid skating on a pond to playing for one of the top teams in the nation."

"But you're thinking of leaving?"

He hadn't said that, but she'd evidently read between the lines. Brooks jerked his shoulders in a shrug. "I don't know. I'm not sure my heart is in it anymore. I don't know if I can get back out there, if I can play the way I need to play to continue to merit being considered a pro, without knowing she's there cheering me on."

Aspen took his hand and squeezed. For a long moment, they sat in silence. She didn't try to say anything to diminish his feelings. She just sat with him in the grief. That empathy was a powerful thing.

The arrival of their food broke the moment, and he wondered where she'd steer the conversation next.

After their server disappeared again, Aspen lifted her gaze back to his. "I lost my mom about ten years ago. Also fast. I was a senior in high school. She went to the doctor for a checkup, and three weeks later she was dead."

"Jesus." Brooks hadn't even known his mom was sick, and that had been horrible. But what Aspen described might've been worse.

"It wrecked me and my dad." She said it in a quiet, matter-of-fact tone. "I skipped my prom to spend time with her in her last days. I didn't go on my senior trip. I ended up not leaving home for college. I switched to an online program, because I couldn't see leaving him on his own. And I've spent the last decade afraid of everything—of something happening to my dad of... I don't know. Starting anything and then losing it."

She shook her head with a wry smile. "My mom would be so pissed if she knew I'd done this. In fact, I'm reasonably sure she's looking down from heaven going, 'Girl, what the hell are you doing with your life?' Which is part of what this trip is about. She begged me not to wait on life. Not to put things off. And that's all I've done since she died."

This time he was the one who took her hand. "Can I ask what changed your mind? What inspired this whole trip?"

She was quiet for a minute. "My dad's just re-married a really lovely woman. He's moving away to where she lives, a few hours away, and left me the house, and... It just felt like it was now or never. He's moving on with his life. I need to move on with mine and figure out what that looks like." Her fingers tightened in his. "Right now, that looks like spending a week at an incredible resort, with a really amazing guy that I didn't see coming."

Brooks thought he understood a little better where she was coming from and why she was doing what she was doing. He could absolutely help her with that. He *wanted* to help her with that, however he could. And he had a good notion of where to start.

Stroking a thumb along the back of her hand, he smiled. "Well, then how about we start that living by finishing this incredible meal and you leave the rest to me?"

6

Aspen didn't think anything of the fact that Brooks excused himself during their meal. She assumed he'd gone to the restroom, either because nature was calling or he needed a few minutes' break from the discussion, which had, admittedly, gotten a lot heavier than the easy flirtation they'd been enjoying before. But the self-satisfied expression he wore when he settled back into his seat raised her curiosity.

"What?"

"What what?" he parroted.

She circled a finger toward his face. "What is this look? You look like you've been sneaking."

"Sneaking? Why, whatever do you mean?"

Humor underscored his attempt at maintaining innocence.

"You're up to something."

He forked up another bite of steak. "I have no idea what you're talking about."

"Uh huh. The same way you had no idea how we ended up with the VIP package at the Empire State Building? I know that was you. Somehow."

"And if it was?" he challenged.

If it was, that was simply further proof that he was such a very good, sweet man.

"You didn't have to do that."

"Since I didn't actually *do* anything but watch you enjoy yourself immensely, I maintain I have no idea what you're talking about."

"Right." But Aspen let the subject drop. She understood that whatever he'd done this time, she wouldn't find out about it until he was good and ready.

That turned out to be not long after they finished dinner. A small box came along with their check—which just got charged to their cabin. Aspen made a mental note to talk to him later about how they'd handle the splitting of expenses on that front.

"What's that?"

"You'll see," he insisted. "C'mon. We have somewhere to be."

"We do?"

"We do."

When he held out his hand, she took it, willing to play along with whatever he had in mind. This whole fake engagement was meant to be an adventure, after all.

They strolled companionably from the main lodge, back toward the lake. The sun hung low in the sky, not yet setting, but offering a stunning backdrop to the water. The golden hour. Its light seemed to limn everything in a gorgeous glow that felt a little like magic. Or maybe that was the company she found herself in.

Aspen noted other guests making their way toward a large building that ran alongside a long pier. As they neared, faint strains of music thumped from within. Brooks steered her in that direction, the little box tucked into his other hand. Not until they were just outside the doors did he stop and extend it.

"Here. You're going to need this."

Brimming with curiosity, Aspen opened it to find... Well, she wasn't entirely sure what she was looking at. It appeared to be a cluster of flowers made from pipe cleaners.

"It's a corsage," Brooks added. "Can't do prom without one."

Aspen's heart gave a little swoop. "Prom? I don't understand."

"Turns out, they have a dance to open every camp session. I know it's not quite the same, without the tux and fancy dress and limo ride, but I thought you might enjoy the vibe."

The swoop turned into a veritable swoon. Less than an hour and a half. He'd known about her missed prom for less than ninety minutes, and he'd gone out of his way to find a way to give some of it back to her.

Aspen's eyes stung. "This is... really above and beyond, Brooks."

He plucked the corsage from the box and began to fasten it to her wrist, his fingers gentle as they brushed her skin. "What kind of fiancé would I be if I didn't romance you from time to time?"

It felt as if he'd been romancing her almost from the moment they'd met. As she looked up into those bright blue eyes, noting the smile lines at the corners, she wished for a few insane seconds that this wasn't a ruse. That they'd have more time than this week. That he'd be a part of her everyday. Because, God, he was everything she'd been missing in her life.

Moved beyond words, she laid the corsage-be-decked hand against his chest, right over his clearly enormous heart, and rose to her toes to brush her lips over his in gratitude. "You are an unbearably sweet man. What will that do for your reputation on the ice?"

"Not a thing. You're the only one who's getting sweet from me."

Aspen had a feeling his mom had been on the receiving end of that sweetness. Which made her a lucky woman before she'd passed. What did it mean that he was sharing it with Aspen now? They weren't strangers anymore. Couldn't be called that after the time they'd spent together. She didn't know exactly what they were. Just... more than they had been.

Don't overthink it.

Her mother's voice echoed through her mind, shutting off the mental spiral that might have robbed some of the joy in the moment.

Aspen took Brooks's hand. "Well, then, you'd better come dance with me."

The long building turned out to be a boathouse. She could see evidence of that underneath the dozens of ropes of cafe lights. A bar had been set up in one corner of the big room, with a couple dozen small tables lining the perimeter, where guests stood and talked and drank. But most were on the dance floor in the middle, twisting and gyrating to the N'Sync song currently blasting from the speakers.

"Honestly, we're mostly just missing the balloon arch," Brooks observed.

She glanced up at him through her lashes. "A vital part of the prom experience?"

"I mean, that and the spiked punch. Do you want a drink?"

Her lips twitched. "Trying to get out of dancing?"

He flattened a hand against his chest. "I would never."

"*Can* you dance?" A lot of guys couldn't or wouldn't. At least, that had been her experience back in high school.

With a look of utter defiance, he took one step backward onto the dance floor and promptly burst into the "Bye Bye Bye" choreography. Several other guests cheered and clustered around to join him for an impromptu dance party. Aspen threw back her head and laughed, absolutely delighted with him. She saw more than one phone come out to film it, and reflected that she'd have done so herself if she'd brought hers. Not that she thought she'd forget the sight of him popping and locking or whatever all those dance moves were called.

When the song ended, she grinned and clasped both hands over her chest. "Be still my inner-tween heart. That was very impressive."

Brooks snagged her at the waist as a slow song started. "Had to prove my cred."

Aspen looped her arms around his shoulders, loving the feel of those muscles beneath her palms. "Dare I ask why you know that dance?"

He offered a sheepish shrug. "My mom was a big fan of boy bands. We learned all the dances when I was growing up. Though, admittedly, I usually have to be far more heavily intoxicated to pull any of that out when I'm not in my own living room."

She loved how he talked about his mother, voice full of unselfconscious affection. It was so very clear they'd been close.

Curling her fingers in the hair at his nape, she moved closer. "Thank you for sharing that with me."

One corner of his mouth kicked up. "She'd have gotten a kick out of it."

There was still grief in his eyes, but it was less in the moment. Aspen knew well enough that he hadn't yet turned the corner. Grief would continue to be an unwelcome guest that popped up for a long time to come. But she was glad he was able to talk about her without hurting quite so much for now. Those happy memories were the thing that would keep him afloat in the harder times.

Brooks pulled her a little closer as they swayed. "So, what other unfulfilled prom dreams did you have?"

"I don't know. I haven't really given any thought to prom in years until tonight."

"Was it all about the dress for you, or did you have *plans* with your date for after?" His eyebrow waggle made it very clear what sort of plans he meant.

With the distance of years, she could laugh about it now. "No to the plans. Yes to the dress." The dress made her think of that shopping trip, and her mom's wisdom about strapless bras. And that brought her back to the lump she'd actually forgotten about for whole hours at a time since she'd met this man.

Something must've shown in her expression because Brooks lost some of the teasing edge. "What?"

Determined not to let what was to come ruin what was now, she forced a smile. "Just having a moment to think how much my mom would've liked you. And also how she'd be fully in support of making that kind of post-prom plans now. Since we're reenacting and all."

"Your mom would've been cool with that?" He looked dubious at that pronouncement.

"At eighteen? Probably not. My high school boyfriend was not long-term material. But I'm not eighteen anymore." *And you are definitely long-term material. Even if I don't get to keep you.*

She ignored the pang she felt at that.

His hand shifted a little lower to rest just above the curve of her ass. "I had noticed."

"Good of you."

"Do you want to get out of here?"

"Not just yet. You went to all this trouble to get me a corsage. Seems a shame not to hang out a while." Plus, she was enjoying dancing with him.

"Your wish."

So they stayed. Song after song. Slow and fast and slow again. Aspen couldn't remember the last time she'd been this relaxed and free. Probably before her mom died. If this was what she had to look forward to over the next week, she was an incredibly lucky woman.

The sun had set by the time the dance ended and they made their way back toward their cabin. The night sky was awash with stars, and she stopped beside the lake, throwing her head back to simply take it all in. "So gorgeous."

"Yeah. It is."

But when Aspen glanced over, Brooks was looking at her. It was instinct to move into him. To lift her mouth to meet his in the moonlight. This kiss wasn't the desperation of last night. This was patience and savoring, knowing they had time to simply enjoy. And damn, she was absolutely enjoying every moment with Brooks Hennessy.

She sighed as he eased back. "I'm really glad I said yes."

His fingers were gossamer soft as they stroked the hair back from her face to tuck it behind her ear. "So am I."

UNLIKE THE NIGHT before at their hotel, Brooks didn't pounce on Aspen the moment they were through the door of their cabin. He hadn't missed that slight dimming in her eyes when she'd been talking about her mother. Ten years on, and apparently the grief could still sneak up and attack. He supposed that was good to know for his own long-term recovery. It seemed Aspen had been just as close to her mom as he had been to his.

He didn't doubt that she still wanted him, but it had been a while since the making of those plans on the dance floor, and the tenor between them had changed somehow. He wanted to make sure she was still on board.

"Tired?"

She turned to face him, brows raised. "I have the rest of my life to be tired after this trip."

Brooks skimmed his fingers over the shoulder bared by her dress. "I can get behind that attitude."

Moving past her, he opened the nightstand drawer and pulled out the quartet of electric candles he'd found in his earlier explorations. Switching them on, he set them around the room, checking to make sure that the blinds were drawn and the door was locked. Only then did he come back to where she stood in the center of the room, watching him.

Last night had been full of fevered desperation. They'd filled those hours with as much as they possibly could, and he'd enjoyed every minute. But now they had more time, and Brooks wanted to linger. To lose himself in the taste and scent and sound of her. Now that he understood better what this trip was for her, he wanted to give her more.

Combing back her hair, he bent to press his lips along the lovely line of her throat, trailing slow, nibbling kisses that made her sigh and relax. That was the name of the game. He wanted to seduce her until she was boneless and beyond sated. Then he wanted to do it all over again.

Aspen's hands lifted to his shirt, fingers fumbling open one button, then the next, and the next, until she spread the fabric aside and kissed his bare chest. That lingering touch of her mouth caused his abs to contract. He wanted to feel it lower. But later.

Reaching around to her back, he slowly lowered the zipper of her dress, one centimeter at a time, until he could nudge the narrow straps off her shoulders and watch the fabric slide down her curves to puddle on the floor. She wore pale pink satin and lace. As she wouldn't have had the chance to shop since meeting him, he knew that was purely for herself. He liked that. Liked that she indulged herself in the pretty and the feminine. And he sure as hell appreciated the view himself.

"You're beautiful."

A flush rose in her cheeks, even as she reached out to shove his shirt off his shoulders. "So are you."

Brooks pulled her in again, body to body, chest to chest, and took her mouth in a long, lingering kiss. Her skin was petal soft beneath his hands, quivering at every touch. His blood was slow and molten, pulsing thick in his veins in a primal call of anticipation. Needing more, he flicked open the clasp of her bra and drew it down and away, leaving her breasts free for his attentions.

Bending, he wrapped his tongue around one nipple. Aspen sucked in a harsh breath, her fingers diving into his hair and flexing as he began to suck. Her hips moved against his in an unconscious echo. He wanted to feel that motion against his fingers, his tongue. His cock.

But not yet.

He took his time, worshiping her breasts until he'd learned her every gasp and moan and her knees finally buckled. Only then did he tumble her back onto the bed, fingers catching the waistband of her underwear as she went and drawing them down.

Brooks reached for her, settling between her legs and stroking a finger through the slickness gathered at the apex of her thighs. Her hips bucked, chasing the contact.

"Don't be a tease," she gasped.

"I wouldn't dare." He bent his head to prove it.

The taste of her was intoxicating, and he took his time to savor as he hadn't last night. The little tugs of her fingers in his hair and the sounds she made as he worked her sent jolts of electricity straight down to his dick. When she shot over the edge, crying his name, he wanted to crow like a god.

She was still quaking as he eased back and stripped out of his pants, pulling a condom from his wallet and rolling on. Her eyes were heavy and languorous as he stretched out beside her.

"Doing okay?"

"I'll let you know in a century or two."

Chuckling, Brooks kissed her again, sliding his hand down the slope of her belly to dip between her thighs, finding her still quivering, wet, and ready. Her hips rose to meet his fingers.

"More?"

"God, yes." Her fingers trailed down his chest, tracing the hair that narrowed into a trail. "I don't think I could ever get enough of you."

"Handy. I feel the same." He shifted over her, settling in the cradle of her hips.

Her eyes opened fully as he began to sink slowly into her welcoming heat. They both sighed as he settled fully inside her, and Aspen lifted her hands to his face, a look of wonder on her own. It felt different from before. Last night had been all tongues and teeth and taking. This felt so much more like giving. Of pleasure. Of affection. Of something more he didn't dare put a name to.

Brooks began to move, a slow, steady thrust and retreat. He watched every flicker of expression over her face in the dim light as he drove them both up, chasing every moan and quickening breath. He kept his pace easy, drawing out the bliss, until at last her legs tightened around him, and she erupted. Unable to hold back any longer, he plunged harder and faster. The rippling waves of her orgasm dragged him over the edge, and he spilled all the longing and desire and affection into her.

As they lay tangled together after, both gasping for breath and shuddering with aftershocks, he thought his orgasm should've left him hollowed out and empty. Instead, it had left him feeling unbearably full of emotions he couldn't and wouldn't name.

So he curled his body around hers and languished in the moment instead.

7

Aspen woke to cocooned warmth, with six-foot-plus of man wrapped around her. The light filtering in through the blinds was weak enough that she knew it was stupid early. They'd had another late night, so she ought to try to get some more sleep. But her brain wouldn't switch off.

At least she didn't have anywhere to be this morning, so she could simply lie here and bask. There'd been no opportunity for that yesterday. She'd been too busy freaking out over what the hell the protocol was for a morning after and trying to pack the last of her things without waking him. She hadn't imagined ending up back in his arms.

She hadn't imagined any of this.

For so long, pleasure of any sort had taken a backseat to being healthy and responsible. She'd been afraid of reaching for anything, lest it get yanked away from her again. That had included relationships deeper than friendship. She'd had a couple of guys she'd been intimate with before. Men she'd dated long enough to feel comfortable going to bed with. But they'd both wanted more. Wanted a long-term she hadn't been willing or able to commit to. So there'd been no one in quite some time. That, too, had been about fear.

When she'd planned this trip, she hadn't set out to take a lover. She hadn't ruled out the idea, but certainly, she hadn't anticipated finding herself fake engaged. And she hadn't anticipated liking that lie nearly so much as she did. Maybe because somewhere, deep down, she hadn't believed she'd ever get to that point for real. Maybe, somehow, she'd known she wouldn't get enough time for that. And that made her want to throw herself into this week with Brooks to a degree she never would've allowed herself. Because what if this was as close as she ever got to having a fiancé who loved her for real?

And yet the more she indulged that fantasy, the more likely it was that she'd catch actual feelings. Maybe she was already starting to. Last night had been... different between them. It had felt like so much more than mutual lust. Even laying here with him like this, feeling the weight of his arm around her waist, his big hand splayed across her torso just below her breasts, felt intimate in a way she hadn't anticipated.

She could stay right here for hours. She could, she knew, turn to him and coax him awake with her hands and mouth, starting the day with another round of really stupendous sex. The mere idea of it had her skin starting to hum with arousal, aching for more of his touch. How easily she'd become addicted to it. To him. To the point that she wondered whether he'd want to keep in touch after their week was over.

Because that made her itch between her shoulder blades, she slowly eased herself free of his hold. Indulgence was one thing. Pretending this was something it wasn't was another.

Brooks rolled over into the warm spot she'd vacated but otherwise didn't stir as she rose from the bed. Moving quietly, she pulled on clothes. A run around the lake would be just the thing to loosen up aching muscles and clear her head.

The sun was just cresting the treeline as she started at an easy jog on the trail around Lake

Waawaatesi. Trees blanketed the mountains that rose around her. The twitter of birds and rustle of the leaves overhead were a lovely melody over the baseline thud of her footsteps on the path. As she made her way around the lake, the tension that had grabbed hold of her began to ease.

Of course she wanted to spend more time with Brooks. He was a great guy. Thoughtful, sexy as hell. Their chemistry was off the charts. And they shared something deeper in having both lost their mothers early in life. Membership to a truly shitty club that no one wanted. But they had no future.

She didn't actually know where he lived. Other than mentioning she was from Georgia, she hadn't told him about Cooper's Bend, either. But either way, he was a pro hockey player. Wherever he did that, it wasn't near her. He'd necessarily be on the road a big chunk of the year. She'd absolutely hate that. Not to mention that if things went the way she expected with her biopsy, she wouldn't want him worrying about her. And God, after his mom not even telling him she was sick, how could Aspen even consider getting involved with him for real? The last thing he needed was to lose someone else he cared about. No. Their liaison or affair or whatever this thing was ended when camp was over. They'd both go back to their respective homes, and that would be that.

That had to be that.

She'd have wonderful memories. And he'd, hopefully, be a little close to healed.

She didn't have the right to want more than that.

If she was already halfway to in love with him, that was just the lust talking. He'd overwhelmed her with his charm and good nature. Of course she'd be dazzled by that. She was only human.

But they had most of a week left together. If things continued like this, she was going to be more than half in love by the end. Maybe a fractured heart was just the price she paid for this little adventure when it was all over. A very human pain to remind her that she was alive for however much time she had left.

A few miles and a solid sweat later, Aspen's head was clearer. The sun glinted off the surface of the water, and more guests and staff were moving around the grounds. She stopped in at the grub shack to grab some bottled water and pick up coffees to take back to the cabin in case Brooks wasn't up yet. Snagging a bottle from the cooler, she opened it right where she stood and began to drink.

Another guy stepped past her, snagging a bottle himself. Judging by the way he was dressed, in athletic shorts and a performance T-shirt, he'd also been out for a run. Lifting his bottle in a toast, he flashed a smile and guzzled half the bottle in one go.

"Good morning for a run."

Aspen nodded, pausing for a breath. "Beautiful area for it."

"I saw you on the trail around the lake."

He had? She'd been too much in her own head to notice anyone else.

"You've got great form."

She glanced in his direction, her brain trying to process. Was he... hitting on her? Given the way his gaze seemed to skim her body, lingering on her bare legs, it seemed like maybe he was. Nonplussed, she took her time finishing the water, wondering what to say. She'd just rolled straight out of bed this morning, so she wasn't wearing her ring. Blurting out that she was engaged seemed too bold in case she'd misread the situation.

"How fast is your mile? I'm looking for a new pace challenge."

"My fiancée is too fast for you, pal." Familiar hands curled around her hips from behind in an unmistakably possessive hold.

Aspen instantly relaxed back into Brooks, not caring why he was here, just grateful he'd saved her from a prospectively awkward situation.

The guy took one look at Brooks and went a little pale. "Sorry, man. Didn't know."

Aspen glanced over her shoulder to see Brooks glowering at the guy with a look that would've done a marauding Viking proud. Why was that hot? By the time she looked back, the other runner was beating a hasty retreat.

"Is scaring smaller guys how you prefer to start your morning?" she teased.

The fierceness melted into a cocky grin. "Breakfast of champions." He dipped his head to press a kiss to that spot between her neck and shoulder. "I missed you when I woke up this morning. Thought you'd sleep in after last night."

"I wanted to go for a run."

"That's something I should probably do. Get back into it. I kind of fell off the wagon with my training after... well, everything."

Did that mean he'd decided for sure to go back? She didn't know how to ask him. Didn't want to pressure him if he hadn't made up his mind. And didn't want to tempt herself with the idea that he might choose something else, lest she delude herself into believing that he'd choose her.

When she said nothing, his hands fell away, and he stepped back a bit. "You know, I didn't think about the fact that maybe you came here to find somebody for real. I'd understand if you want to back out of our arrangement." His words said one thing, but the stiff posture of his body said something else entirely.

Aspen kept her tone mild as she looked up at him. "Do I really strike you as somebody who'd be willing to jump straight from your bed into someone else's?"

"No."

"Good. Because I'm not. I'm fine with what we're doing here. I'm fine with temporary." If she kept saying that, she'd start to believe it. Determined to get them back on the right foot, she closed the distance, looping her arms around his neck and pressing close. "And I'm more than fine with you."

The instant relaxation told her that had been the right move. He didn't want to end things between them yet any more than she did.

Brushing a quick kiss over his lips, she dropped back to her feet. "Come on. Let's get some breakfast and figure out what we want to do today."

"WE'RE BEING WATCHED."

At Aspen's words, Brooks looked over at the cluster of other guests utilizing the archery range. There were, indeed, several people staring at the two of them. One even had their phone up to snap a photo.

His temper kindled. Angling his head, he lifted a brow at the woman in a *Really?* gesture. She had the good grace to flush and put the phone back into her pocket.

Brooks was accustomed to this sort of thing. Which didn't mean he liked it, but he'd learned over the years he had to control his reactions lest he end up in the media for simply being human. For the most part, he'd learned to ignore it. This was part of the price he paid for being a somewhat public figure.

But it was clear Aspen was uncomfortable. The relaxed posture that had led to her thoroughly trouncing him in their friendly competition with bows had disappeared. She shot one more glance over her shoulder at the group before refocusing on the target and drawing. On an exhale, she released. The arrow whizzed through the air, hitting the outer ring of the target instead of near the center like all her previous efforts. She made a noise of disgust in the back of her throat.

Brooks was sorry for his role in bringing her into the public eye. Not that he'd have traded a moment of their time together. But he could tell the additional attention was diminishing her enjoyment of the game. That would never do.

"Are you wedded to staying here at camp for the duration, or are you game for a bit of a field trip?"

Aspen turned her attention to him. "What kind of field trip?"

"A surprise." He'd need to get back to camp proper, where there was a better signal, to call and see if it was actually a possibility.

"You're full of those. But okay. I trust you."

And wasn't that a freaking miracle?

They turned their equipment into the attendant at the gear hut and made their way back toward the center of the resort. Just in case, he'd done a little recon on this for his own purposes before he'd come out here. But taking Aspen would be that much more fun.

As soon as he had a signal, he stopped. "Why don't you head on back to the cabin? I'll be right behind you."

"I can't hear your phone call?" Her voice was full of teasing instead of pique.

"As it would ruin the surprise, no, you can't. Go on." He nudged her up the trail.

Crossing her eyes, she stuck her tongue out at him. Damn, she was cute.

Brooks returned the gesture. "Be a good girl and go back to the cabin."

Aspen heaved a put-upon sigh. "Fine. See you in a few."

He waited only long enough to see her get out of earshot before he made the call and asked to speak to the manager. Once the guy came on the line, he explained what he wanted, asking whether it was possible. Assured that it absolutely was, Brooks promised they'd be there within the hour.

Back at the cabin, he found Aspen lounging on the bed, legs crossed. "Put on the warmest clothes you brought."

She stared at him as if he were a lunatic. "You are aware it's July, right? I didn't pack warm clothes."

"Do you have jeans?"

"Yeah."

"Then put those on."

Aspen continued to pepper him with questions all the way out to his G-Wagon.

Brooks firmly refused to say anything but, "You'll see."

When they pulled up in front of the long, windowless building a little over half an hour later, Aspen frowned. "Where are we?"

"Well, I'm going out on a limb here, but given that you didn't have frozen lakes where you grew up, I'm banking that you probably didn't have an opportunity to learn how to ice skate. So I thought I'd teach you."

She blinked. "I say again… it's July?"

Brooks grinned and gestured to the building. "This is an ice rink."

"There are places you can *ice skate* in the *summer?*"

"Careful, Fairchild. Your Southern is showing. Yeah, rinks are a lot more common up north. You can go year round."

"I guess it makes sense that you can't just practice hockey when it's cold outside."

"True enough. We'll have the place to ourselves today." He didn't add that he'd rented the whole facility for the rest of the day to make sure of it.

Sliding out of the SUV, he circled around to

pop the back hatch. He rarely traveled without his gear, so he grabbed his bag and led Aspen inside.

The manager, a middle-aged white man with thinning brown hair and wiry build, was waiting in the entryway. "Mr. Hennessy, so nice to meet you. Miss, welcome to Dinsbrook Memorial Arena."

Aspen was looking everywhere at once, arms wrapped around her middle against the chill. "Thank you."

"She's gonna need fitting in some skates. I brought my own."

"Of course. What's your shoe size?"

She told him, and he disappeared behind the counter to retrieve some skates.

Brooks set down his bag and pulled out one of his jerseys. "C'mere. This will help with the cold."

He tugged the jersey over her head. It hung halfway to her knees, but it would do the trick to keep her warmer on the ice.

Aspen worked her arms through the sleeves and did a little spin. "How do I look?"

A possessive thrill shot through him, seeing her with his name on her back. "Would you think me entirely caveman if I said I really want to see you in this and only this later?"

Her eyes flashed with heat. "Maybe. But I find that works for me."

"Good."

"Here we go!" The manager offered up a pair of skates. "Rink access is just through there, and if you want any concessions, just let me know."

Without taking his eyes off Aspen, Brooks thanked the guy and led her to a bench beside the ice. The small rink was dimly lit but for the lights over the ice that made its surface gleam like a sheet of polished glass. There was little he loved more than being the first blades on a new surface. The tug he felt surprised him. And maybe relieved him a little, too. He hadn't been on the ice at all since that disastrous playoff game. He'd thought maybe all of it had been tainted by his mother's death.

At the reminder, grief socked him in the chest like a sucker punch. He breathed through the ache, focusing on the task at hand. "Sit."

With a smirk of amusement, she did so. "I do know how to tie shoes."

"But you don't know how to tie skates. I'm here to make sure you don't injure yourself." Kneeling at her feet, he removed her shoes, one at a time, and slid the skates on, which felt weirdly intimate. Maybe it was this bubble of isolation he'd arranged after being surrounded by people the last few days. Maybe it was just her and this connection between them.

As if Aspen sensed it too, she reached out to cup his face, stroking her thumb along the curve of his cheek. "Thank you for this."

Brooks leaned into the touch, just a little, soaking up the contact. One corner of his mouth kicked up. "Don't thank me yet until you see if you actually like it."

Tying the laces—tight enough for proper ankle support, but not too tight—he quickly slipped on his own skates, then held out his hands for hers. "Take my forearms. You're gonna want to brace yourself on me as you stand."

Her fingers curled around his arms, and he cupped her elbows, gently bringing her to her feet. She instantly wobbled, her grip tightening with a gasp.

"Don't worry. I'm right here." Brooks helped balance her as he moved the few feet to the ice. "You're just going to step onto the ice as if you're stepping onto any new surface. One foot, then the other." He demonstrated, then waited for her.

She eyed the ice with a little trepidation but gamely stepped onto it... and promptly flailed like a baby deer, falling into his arms. He wrapped around her, enjoying the weight of her against him. "Whoa there. I've got you."

Gasping, she shot a narrow-eyed glare at him. "I think that was a move."

He carefully lifted her straight again and grinned. "So what if it was?"

She grinned back. "Good thing I like you."

"Good thing. If you liked that one, you're gonna really like this." He slid his arm around her waist to stabilize and guide her movements. "Now, skating is all about balance and confidence." With a few easy movements, he had them gliding slowly along the edge of the rink.

Her first strides were clumsy, her feet awkwardly shuffling as they tried to match his.

"Bend your knees a bit, and keep your weight centered over the blades."

"Like this?"

"Better. Now, loosen up. You're not the Tin Man here."

Gradually, her initial stiffness gave way to more fluid motion, and she laughed—part nerves, part joy—as she experienced the sensation of gliding properly for the first time. The sound warmed something deep inside him that had been chilled beyond measure for longer than he wanted to think about.

Wanting to see her face, he pivoted, shifting his hold to both of her hands and matching her rhythm.

"You're going backwards! How are you going backwards?"

He grinned again. "I've got twenty-five years of practice. This is above your pay grade for now. Keep on doing what you're doing."

They circled the rink, slowly picking up a little bit more speed, and Aspen's movements became more confident.

"You wanna try it on your own?"

"Okay." Her voice trembled a little, but her expression was determined.

So Brooks released her, continuing to skate backwards, pacing her.

Delight lit her face when she didn't fall. "I'm doing it! I'm doing it!"

"Hell, yeah, you are!"

She put on a little bit more speed. "I think maybe I've got this."

That declaration was the kiss of death. Abruptly, she stumbled, her feet coming straight out from under her so that she crashed onto the ice with a shriek.

Brooks closed the distance in an instant. "Shit! You okay?"

Aspen looked up at him from where she lay on her butt and laughed. "Toe pick!"

Assured she wasn't seriously injured, he let himself join her with a chuckle. "My mom loved that movie, too."

"Someone had to say it. It was practically a moral imperative."

The grief slammed into him again, harder this time. A parade of memories scrolled through his brain of the hundreds of times he'd skated with his mother. On the pond. At countless ice rinks across the country. She'd loved skating almost as much as he'd loved hockey.

"Brooks?" Aspen's quiet voice pulled him out of the emotional quicksand.

He realized she held out her hand, waiting to be pulled up.

This was why he'd been so determinedly focused on her. When he did, there was less room for the grief. Even sharing things about his mom hurt less with Aspen, because it was so very clear she got it.

Lodging his brain firmly in the present, on her, he lifted her to her feet, and they continued the lesson. He taught her how to stop and start, how to turn, and eventually even how to fall safely, which resulted in both of them in a laughing heap on the ice. All of it was an excuse to keep his hands on her.

Not that he needed the excuse since, for the purposes of the next week, Aspen was his fiancée. Right now, she belonged to him. As the day wore on, though, he couldn't stop himself from reflecting on how natural and right it felt to be with her. Couldn't stop wishing that it wasn't temporary. Because he liked Aspen. He liked being with her. Liked who he was with her.

Was it truly Aspen herself? Or was it simply that he was so desperate for a distraction, and she happened to be tailor made as the perfect one? Feeling more than a little guilty over the idea of that, he doubled down on his efforts to charm her.

It was, after all, the least he could do.

8

"I shouldn't have sat down." Aspen didn't even try to hide the fact that she was rubbing at the sore muscles of her ass. "I think between the ice skating and the bed, I've worked out more in the past few days than I have in months. At least using muscles that don't normally get used."

"It gets better with practice," Brooks insisted.

She shot him a glance. "Which? The skating or the... other things."

He paused, then smirked. "Both."

"God bless practice. But I'd bless it more if I had access to a hot tub. Or at least a super hot shower. I'm not sure I've thawed out from the rink yet." She'd fallen so much that, by the end, she and the ice had been intimately acquainted. But it had been a truly fantastic day. He had, yet again, gone to all this trouble to give her new memories and an experience she certainly wouldn't have had on her own.

"If they have a hot tub, I don't know about it. But we could head back to the cabin for a hot shower—"

"I notice you're using the singular there."

"Very observant of you." He winked and swung their joined hands. "But I actually have a better idea."

"Oh really? Well, those continue to turn out well for me, so lead the way."

"We do need to stop by the cabin first to pick something up."

"Okay."

The something ended up being a couple of towels. He stuffed them in a backpack and slung it over one shoulder before leading her back out of the cabin and into the woods. As the sun was close to setting, the shadows of the trees stretched long, lending an eerie twilight to the area.

"If this were a different kind of story, you'd be taking me to where you hide the bodies."

Brooks looked down at her. "Oh, that took a dark turn."

"But," she qualified, "it's not that kind of story."

"No?"

"Absolutely not." She might not know much about Brooks, but she knew he was a good man and no threat to any part of her. Well, except her heart.

"What kind of story is it?"

With his hand warm around hers and all the memories they'd made spinning through her mind, she admitted the truth to herself.

It's a love story. God help me, it's a love story.

But she couldn't say that.

Copping out, she shrugged and offered a smile. "To be determined."

He gave her some side-eye, like he knew that wasn't what she really meant, but he didn't call her on it.

Aspen had no idea how far they'd walked before she began hearing some sort of dull roar. "What is that?"

"Well, if I followed the directions I was given correctly, we should be coming up on Firefly Falls, for which the camp is named."

"Oh! I didn't realize it was a real place." Then

again, she hadn't looked too deeply into the history of the camp when she'd booked her stay.

"It's supposed to be."

"I'm surprised the trail isn't marked."

"I think that's the point. To keep it hidden and special for those in the know. If we're lucky, I timed this right."

"For what?"

"You'll see."

A hundred or so yards later, the trail opened up and Aspen gasped. The falls themselves thundered down into a wide pool maybe fifty or sixty feet across. The pool was wrapped on both sides by rock that ended with only a narrow gap to allow the water to keep on flowing into Lake Waawaatesi. Thick trees crowded around all sides, lending a sense of total privacy. And everywhere she looked were fireflies. Hundreds of them winking in synchrony in the last dying light of the sun.

"It's gorgeous," she breathed. "I've never seen this many at once. Especially outside the South. It's magical."

"Timed it right for sure." Brooks stripped off his shirt.

"What are you doing?"

"Going swimming."

"Oh, but I didn't bring my swimsuit."

He grinned at her. "Neither did I." In one quick move, he shucked his pants and strode, gloriously naked, into the water.

Aspen had never been skinny dipping. Shocker. But the entire point of this trip was to rack up experiences, so she stripped down to the buff and went to join him.

"Eeep! The water's cold!" Gooseflesh rose along her skin the moment her feet were covered.

"You gotta get out here to the middle, where the trees didn't block the sun."

"Okay, I'm trusting you. But it's on you to warm me up if you're lying."

"That is a duty I swear to take very seriously."

Taking a breath, she made a shallow dive fully into the water, hurriedly stroking out to where he treaded water.

Surfacing beside him, she swiped the hair back from her face. "Okay, you were right. This is better." Tipping her head back, she stared up at the stars winking on in the darkening sky. "So beautiful."

"Worth the hike, for sure."

She moved her arms back and forth, kicking

gently to stay afloat. "I'm pretty tired. I don't know how long I'll be able to make it, but I will absolutely give it the old college try."

His arms came around her, eliminating the need to kick. "I've got you. We can stay out here as long as you like."

On a contented sigh, she laid her head back against his shoulder. She was aroused. They were naked together in arguably one of the most romantic spots in the area. Of course she was aroused. But in the moment, it was more of a pleasant undercurrent. It was enough to be held close, skin to skin, basking in nature and each other. This was another of the mile long list of things she didn't think she could ever get enough of, even if more than this week was on the table. Which she knew it wasn't.

Turning her head, she brushed a kiss to his jaw —the only part of him she could reach without turning around. "Thank you for today. It was so incredibly fun, and I'm never going to forget it."

Brooks pressed a kiss to her shoulder, as he frequently did. It was a small gesture, but one that would be burned into her memories every bit as much as all these big ones he'd given her. "It was fun to teach you."

"Tell me what you love about it. Skating. Hockey. All of it." Maybe if she could remind him why he loved the sport, it would help him make the decision whether to go back. Going back was probably the right choice for him. If he left now, it would be purely out of grief, and she thought he'd probably regret it.

He was quiet for a long moment, resting his cheek against her hair as they both continued watching the light show. "I love the freedom of being on the ice. And I love the challenge. There's always room to improve skills, whether that's skating, puck handling, shooting. I love the physical exertion. It's hella good stress relief. And of course, I love the camaraderie and the teamwork. Those guys are my brothers."

"Was it some of your teammates who sent you here?"

"Yeah. They thought I was wallowing too much and that it would do me good to get the hell outta Dodge, as it were. Can't argue that they weren't right."

"I'm certainly lucky they sent you. You'd mentioned you were struggling with whether to go back. If you decided to leave the sport, what would you do instead?"

"I don't know. I never truly considered doing anything else with my life."

"Well, what else do you love?"

He considered that for a long while before shifting his hold, spinning her in his grip to face him. For a potent moment, he stared down at her, his hand stroking the wet hair back from her face. "I don't know. But right now, I'm loving being here with you."

Aspen's heart began to pound. He wasn't saying he loved her. That would be ridiculous. But they were coming to matter to each other, and that was a lot.

Sliding her hands over his shoulders, she whispered, "Me too."

Then he kissed her again, and she forgot that she'd ever been cold.

～

"YOU LOOK like you're thinking deep thoughts."

Brooks glanced over at Aspen in the kayak next to his. "Guess I am."

"Want to share with the class, or would you rather keep it to yourself?"

"I'm not contemplating state secrets or anything. Just thinking about what you asked me last night, about what else I love besides hockey, and what the hell I'd do with my life if I retire. When I suggested to Grady and Colter—those are two of my teammates—that I might just quit the whole damned thing, I hadn't given any thought at all to what the hell I'd do instead. I mean, I don't have to find anything immediately. I've been paid well for the time I've played." He broke off, catching her eye again. "I guess it's a little rude to say that."

Aspen jerked her shoulders. "I assumed you were making more than pennies by playing at your level. You couldn't have pulled off some of the surprises for me if you didn't have some kind of money. That just means you have a safety net. Presuming you aren't the kind of guy to just blow it all."

"No, I've been responsible with it. Growing up with a single mom, it was definitely important to me that there be savings. The only thing I really spent excessively on—according to her anyway— was the fact that as soon as I was able, I bought her a house and a new car. And airfare so she could come see me play whenever she wanted."

"Wanting to take care of her after she took care of you all those years is hardly excessive."

"That's what I said." And Brooks could still remember the stunned delight on his mom's face when he'd presented her with that house, even as she'd said it was too much. Nothing would ever have been too much for her.

Shaking off the memory, he dragged his brain back to the conversation. "Anyway, I haven't given any real thought to what I'd do other than hockey. I've never done anything else. Never *wanted* to do anything else."

"Don't a lot of retired sportsball players end up as commentators or whatever?"

"I wouldn't really be into that even if someone offered it. It would mean I was still around the game I don't want to be around because it hurts. That's fundamentally what all of it is about. I love it, and it also hurts. That's why I'm even thinking about leaving. Is that crazy?"

"No. Grief is a powerful thing. And right now, you're still riding the leading edge of it. I'd love to tell you that it will fade. To some extent, it will. But it's not that you ever really get over it. You just learn how to live with it. You're the only one who can parse out whether this is a matter of the grief overshadowing everything else or if it's permanently tainted the sport for you. And that's not likely an easy question to answer."

"No." Brooks sat with that for a bit. "A big part of why it hurts is because much as I love hockey, it's the thing that took me away from her. It was the reason I wasn't there. The reason she didn't tell me she was sick. She didn't want to impact my career. So in a sense, I feel like hockey robbed me of my last possible time with her."

Aspen looked out over the lake, clearly considering. "If you were something else—I don't know... a traveling salesman or corporate something or other who was frequently on the road for work— would you feel the same way? Is it the job itself? Or is it that you feel guilty because you were doing something you love?"

Damn, she wasn't pulling punches. "I don't know how to answer that."

"Let's shift gears into brainstorming, then. Do you have training to do anything else?"

"No. I didn't go to college. I got into the AHL when I was a wet-behind-the-ears eighteen and never looked back."

"Do you have any interest in college? Studying something else? Doing something completely different?"

"Honestly, I can't imagine sitting still that long."

"Fair. You lead a very active life, and there is a lot of butt-in-chairing involved in school."

He studied her as she dipped her paddle

smoothly into the water, gently propelling herself forward. "What do you do?" He realized this was the first time it had occurred to him to ask.

"I've got a degree in business, technically. But I have a little shop for planner stuff."

"Planner stuff?"

"I design custom calendar and planner spreads, stickers, habit trackers, and other organizational tools."

"Really? That's a big thing?" Brooks couldn't wrap his brain around that. "Don't people just go down to Target and buy a pre-printed one?" As soon as the words were out, he wished he could bite his tongue. That had sounded incredibly dismissive.

But Aspen only laughed. "Yes, planners are big business."

"Huh. I guess I'm not really a planner person. I don't have to be. I have people to tell me where I'm supposed to be and when."

She grinned. "It's not for everyone. But for the people who are into it... yeah, they spend a lot to organize their lives."

"I guess I can see that. Some people would pay a lot in the name of taking control of their lives."

"True enough. I'm not making pro hockey

money—whatever that is—but I make a living, and I enjoy what I do."

He imagined she had some kind of little shop somewhere. Something neat and tidy, where she used all that Southern charm to lead customers to the thing that would best suit their needs. Even as the image bloomed in his mind, an odd disappointment filtered through him.

She had a business established. One she clearly loved. He couldn't imagine asking her to even think of leaving that for him.

Startled at the thought, Brooks stopped paddling. Shit. Was he actually thinking of asking her if she'd be willing to *move*? For him? That was utterly ridiculous and selfish of him. He couldn't say they barely knew each other. Not anymore. But it had only been a matter of days. It would be lunacy to ask that of her.

But... if he was considering retiring and doing something else... he could do that something else wherever she was. He hadn't spent much time in Georgia, but surely he could find something to do. Wouldn't it be worth trying it to find out if this thing between them was more than a mere distraction?

"Want to break for a swim?"

Aspen's voice pulled him out of his contemplation.

"Sure."

They beached their kayaks in a nearby cove, well down the shore from camp proper, then waded into the water again. As if magnetized, he automatically reached for her, tugging her close. Aspen cuddled in, running her hands over his chest and shoulders in obvious appreciation.

"So, you're pretty strong."

"Yeah." Brooks didn't miss the twinkle in her eyes. "What are you thinking?"

"Strong enough to prospectively do the lift from *Dirty Dancing?*"

Her hopeful expression had him laughing. "Why?"

She gestured expansively. "I mean, look at where we are! It feels like another one of those moral imperatives."

"Wasn't that movie set in the Catskills?"

"Yeah, but we're close enough. So?"

"Well, that's going to depend on your abs. I can lift your weight, no problem. But that particular move would require a lot of core strength. We can certainly try it here in the water, at least."

The pursuit of fulfilling her latest fantasy took

up all of his concentration as he worked to lift her over his head. The process involved a lot of laughter and splashing and straight up fun. That was something there'd been very little of in his life lately. There'd been grief and there'd been hockey. Which used to be fun, and probably would still be fun on some level. But it was also work. Being with Aspen like this reminded him he needed more than that.

"Okay, okay. We're gonna get it this time." She braced herself, then took off running toward him through the water and leaping at the last second.

He caught her around the waist and lifted, and this time she didn't over rotate and didn't collapse. Her arms spread wide and her body held stiff as he braced her over his head. She sang a few off-key bars of "I've Had the Time of My Life." Then she took a nosedive into the water that toppled him as well.

Brooks came up sputtering to find her grinning in utter delight.

"We did it! Only for a few seconds, but it counts!"

"Hell yeah, we did!"

This woman made him happy. Pure and simple.

He knew his mom would love that and exactly what she'd say about what he should do.

Which meant he had a whole different problem. Because now that he'd been reminded of how much he loved being on the ice and how much he loved the game, he was thinking about going back.

But he was still thinking about leaving his career, not because of grief, but because of something that felt a whole lot like love.

9

"In the wake of the storm, the mansion seemed utterly deserted. No lights. No movement. Nothing. It was like the family had vanished into thin air. Well, the townsfolk, thinking maybe the Hathaways had been hurt, headed out to check on them. The night was much like this one, cloudy, with a half moon and a little bite to the air. When they arrived, the front door was ajar."

Aspen leaned toward Brooks as she settled on a log with a roasting stick and a bag of marshmallows. "So we're telling ghost stories now?"

"Seems like," he murmured.

Not exactly her preferred form of entertainment, but she'd tolerate it in the name of s'mores.

After all the time on the lake today, she deserved at least two.

"They shoved the door open with a mighty creak that seemed to echo well beyond the house, and when they stepped inside, everything was shrouded in darkness and silence. No one answered their calls. Thinking something most foul had happened to the family, they began to climb the grand staircase. And suddenly, a chill wind gusted through the house, dousing their lanterns and leaving them in the pitch black."

As if to echo the point, a breeze kicked up, making their own fire dance. Aspen shuddered despite herself, barely remembering to rotate her marshmallow before it caught fire. Brooks scooted closer, wrapping an arm around her, as if he sensed her discomfort.

"And in the dark came a soft, haunting melody from somewhere in the depths of the mansion. The brave among them followed the music to the grand ballroom, where a figure sat at at the piano, fingers wringing a tune from the instrument so mournful it made every man among them weep. And as they watched, the clouds parted so moonlight streamed through the window illuminating the musician as she lifted her head and looked at them with hollow, soulless eyes."

Aspen's hand shook just a little as she squashed her marshmallow between two slabs of graham cracker and a piece of chocolate. Why did they always have to go with the creepy stuff? Why not romantic stories?

"One of the party stepped forward, reaching out toward the woman who could be none other than Eliza Hathaway, but as he did, she vanished, as did the music. In an instant, the room turned to ice, and a voice whispered, 'Leave... now...'"

Brooks' breath was warm against her ear. "We don't have to stay."

She leaned into him, focusing on the warmth of his arm and his solid presence beside her. It was stupid to be freaked out by a story. The guy was probably just making it up on the spot. But truth was, she hated this stuff. She hadn't even been able to watch the spoof of *The Exorcist* without having nightmares.

"I'm fine. I want my s'mores."

"Let me know if that changes."

Aspen bit into her s'more, appreciating how Brooks seemed to *see* her in a way no one else ever had. What a gift that was. He understood without having to be told that she wasn't comfortable and sought to do something about it. Sweet man.

"Well, you can bet your ass they ran hell for

leather out of that mansion. But as they looked back at the house from the relative safety of the forest, they saw Eliza at the window, watching them with eerie blue eyes that glowed in the dark." The storyteller sat back. "The Hathaway mansion never was occupied after that, and it fell into disrepair. But they say Eliza's spirit still haunts those ruined halls. Hikers sometimes hear a lonely piano echoing through the hills. So, when you're out here in the Berkshires, if you ever hear the faint strains of the ivories... remember the tragic tale of Eliza Hathaway, and whatever you do, don't follow the music."

As the speaker sat back, letting the crackle of the fire punctuate the end of the story, Brooks shifted, scooping Aspen onto his lap. She cuddled in, not truly afraid but appreciating the closeness, nonetheless. Finishing her first s'more, she let him help her add another marshmallow to the end of her stick and extended it over the fire to toast.

It was yet another memory she'd have of him. There were so many now. It felt greedy to want more. Yet, here she was. Tipping her head to his, she let herself indulge in the "What if?" What if she went back home and Linnea was right? What if the biopsy revealed that there was a completely benign reason for the lump? What if she didn't have cancer? What if it turned out she had a whole lot more tomorrows?

Would Brooks consider spending them with her?

That didn't feel like a reasonable thing to ask him. Certainly not without knowing the truth about her condition. She refused to bring up the potential for cancer with him. They didn't have that kind of relationship. This hazy, potential future wasn't a thing she'd even consider pursuing without having an answer.

But as she sat warming herself by the fire, she let herself consider the possibility that there could be a future. And she allowed herself to actually want it. To want him beyond this week. Beyond the farce of their engagement.

He hadn't yet decided what he was doing about his career, but if he went back to hockey, the reality was that it wouldn't be in Georgia. There was no hockey in Georgia, so far as she knew. If there was, he'd have mentioned it. Which meant that if she wanted to pursue this, it would mean leaving Georgia herself. Leaving the house and those memories of her mother it represented.

That was no small thing and triggered a cascade of potential grief she wasn't prepared to deal with.

No sense in going down that path right now. She couldn't allow herself to give in to the hope of a future. Not without having all the information. No matter what hurdles she'd overcome, she wasn't brave enough to do that. But she acknowledged to herself that if there was a chance, she'd love to take it with him. Because he'd be worth it. She suspected he'd be worth everything.

"Had enough s'mores?"

"Yeah. I think two is enough for me. I'm not quite ready to go back to the cabin." There'd be better lighting there, and he might realize something was wrong. Not that anything was wrong, exactly. Not that she could tell him or would tell him, given how close his own grief over his mom's loss still was.

"We'll have a walk then. Let dessert settle."

Which was how she found herself strolling along the lake, tucked close to his side.

"Did you always live in Georgia?" he asked.

"I did. Born and raised."

"Do you like it there?"

"Love it. I'm a creature of the South, for sure. I've lived in the same house most of my life."

"Even now?"

"Even now. My dad remarried a few weeks

ago, right before I took this trip. He gifted me with the house because he's moving in with his new wife."

"Lotta memories there, I imagine."

"Yeah. Deep roots. What about you? You said you grew up in Michigan?"

"Yeah."

"Big city or small town?"

"Some of both. We moved around a bit. Spent a lot of time in the towns on the outskirts of Grand Rapids. But I left for my hockey career, and Mom followed me."

"Do you ever want to go back?"

"No. Mom's house is—was—near where I landed. There's nothing left for me there."

Aspen couldn't imagine being that kind of rootless. Did he feel unmoored? His mom had clearly been his anchor. She'd been his home. Not a place. With her gone, he was bound to feel emotionally adrift, whether he'd acknowledge that to himself or not.

Aspen found herself wondering if life could possibly work out in such a way that she could share her roots with him. She wanted to give that to him. Not that it would be an option if he continued to play hockey. He'd have to retire, and she'd never ask that of him. Ending his hockey career was a decision he'd have to make on his own, with zero pressure.

And why was she even obsessing over this? She herself wouldn't know for probably several more weeks whether she had the possibility of a future, and she didn't know how to handle it. If they maintained contact after camp and the news was the worst, how could she possibly tell him? And yet, not telling him would be tantamount to ghosting him when she died. Both routes would hurt him, and that was the absolute last thing she wanted to do.

Maybe better to keep this to herself. Then, if she got a reprieve, she could find a way to contact him. They hadn't swapped contact information at this point. There'd been no need since they'd essentially been joined at the hip. But he was more or less a public figure. She could find a way. More, she wanted to find a way because he represented the potential for a future she hadn't even known she wanted. She just had to find the guts to reach for it.

～

BROOKS TRIED to doze as the hammock rocked gently in the breeze. He was alone for the first time in days, Aspen having availed herself of a massage at the spa. Not that he wouldn't have been up for a couple's massage, but he'd gotten the sense she wanted a little time to herself. They'd spent practically every waking—and sleeping—minute together since their arrival, so that was more than fair, considering she'd booked this trip solo.

But he was twitchy being away from her. Their week together was counting down, and he didn't want it to end. He didn't want to go back to his empty, lonely house in Colorado. Didn't want to go back to an empty bed. It wasn't the sex—although that had been outstanding. It was just... her. He'd accepted she was more than a distraction or a comfort. She'd absolutely become a friend. And Brooks was pretty sure she had the potential to be a whole hell of a lot more. But he had to decide what to do about it.

She was attracted to him. That wasn't a question. And he knew she'd grown fond of him. But did she still see him as a time-limited commitment? One giant live-in-the-moment experience that she was enjoying *because* there was an expiration date? Or was she also wanting more?

Logistics were a thing. The reality was that she lived in Georgia, and he lived in Colorado. For now, anyway. By the time this trip was over, it was possible the general manager would already have made arrangements to trade him God-knew where. Could be closer to her. Could be even further. Chances were, it would be long distance either way if he elected to continue his hockey career. Long distance was hard under the best of circumstances, and with all the months he'd be on the road in addition to the long distance thing, the time they'd be able to truly spend together would likely be little and far between. Was it even fair to ask her to consider that?

Brooks wanted to believe that if he mattered enough to her, that they could make that work. But he wasn't sure he was ready to find out that he didn't matter as much to her as she did to him. And if he posed this question, there was a very good chance that might be the answer.

But there was still a good chance that she felt as he did—like this whole crazy trip was the start of something real and lasting, if only they could sort out the details.

When his phone rang, he almost ignored it. The past few days of no contact with the outside world had been glorious. But just in case...

Grady's name flashed across the display.

"Hey, man. What's up?"

"Dude, I legit didn't really think you'd answer. You've gone incommunicado again."

"I'm on vacation." Never mind the fact that the last time he'd gone radio silent on his friends had been because he'd been so deeply mired in the well of grief they'd basically had to send a search party after him.

"Uh huh." Grady's tone was dry. "And how is your 'engagement' going?"

Brooks couldn't see his hands, but he could hear the air quotes around engagement in the tone alone. "It's going great. We're having a really good time. She's awesome."

Grady paused. "Awesome as in a she's-a-really-great-lay-and-a-stress-relief kind of way or in a you're-gonna-want-to-pursue-this-past-this-week kind of way?"

Brooks bristled. "She's not just someone I'm sleeping with. Have some respect."

"Sorry, man. I'm not trying to offend. I'm literally just asking a question. It's relevant."

"Why exactly is this any of your business?"

"Apart from the fact that I'm your friend, we've got news."

"News about what?"

"We heard who they're looking to potentially trade you to."

Any pretense of relaxation evaporated. Brooks dropped one leg out of the hammock to stop the sway and braced himself. "Okay, who are the options?"

"Vegas, Tampa, and prospectively that new team they're forming in Atlanta."

Brooks blinked. "Atlanta? Isn't this like the third time they've tried to build a team there?" He dimly remembered hearing rumblings about them getting approval, but hadn't paid much attention. He was sure as shit paying attention now.

"Yeah. And I have no idea how successful they'll be this go-round. But it's on the list. It seemed like something you ought to know so you could put in your vote with the GM. Given what you've just said, it seems like Atlanta might be the best fit for you."

"Why?" Brooks knew why. It would be closer to Aspen. But given the potential for a new team crashing and burning there—again—why did his friend think it was the best idea?

"Well, I just thought that, given how things are going with Aspen, you'd want to be closer to her."

Hearing his own thoughts come out of Grady's mouth, Brooks felt a bit of a chill. "I never told you her name, and I definitely never told you where she was from."

The silence went on too long. With every second that passed, the ball of lead in Brooks' gut got heavier.

"Dude, it's out there."

"What do you mean, 'It's out there'?"

"The press have found out who she is. They're talking about her in the media. Talking about both of you, making all kinds of speculation."

Brooks needed to be very, very sure he understood. "You mean they've got her full name and where she's from?" Hell, he didn't even know where in Georgia she was from.

"Yeah. You didn't know?"

"Fuck no, I didn't know. I've been staying off the internet entirely."

"Well, you may want to go check that out and have a conversation with Rebekah to see if there's anything you need to get ahead of."

He wanted to believe that if there was, she'd have already contacted him, but he knew well enough he couldn't be certain.

"I haven't paid that much attention to everything," Grady qualified. "I don't know that there's anything disrespectful or problematic, but your lady might need some warning."

"Fuuuuuuuck." Brooks blew out a long breath. He'd known this was a possibility. A probability, even. He'd just hoped that there'd be more time. That the vultures would leave him be and wouldn't try to horn in on another aspect of his life, and thus, hers.

"Yeah, this is something I absolutely need to take care of. Thanks for letting me know."

"Of course, man. Either way, wherever you end up going, we're really gonna miss you."

"Yeah, me too. You're a good friend, Grady. Thanks."

Brooks hung up and immediately opened a browser. He had to find out exactly what degree of horrible he had to break to his fake fiancée.

10

By the time Aspen made it out of her massage, she'd determined that it was a luxury worth tweaking her monthly budget to accommodate. She felt loose and relaxed and very Zen. The masseuse had even managed to do away with the aches she'd still felt from her ice skating lesson. Blissful.

Because she still had another fifteen or twenty minutes until she was meant to meet Brooks at the grub shack for some lunch, she decided it was a good time to check in on everything back home. Her dad and Tricia were due back from their honeymoon soon, and she hadn't actually even looked at Linnea's texts in days because she'd been so focused on Brooks. Not that she thought her friend would have a problem with that, but... well, Aspen hadn't actually *told* her about Brooks, because that was complicated and chances were, Linnea would ask the hard questions she didn't yet have answers for.

Hitting the lakeside trail, she checked her phone. There were blessedly few notifications that had to be dealt with, but a voicemail from a number she didn't know caught her attention.

"Miss Fairchild. This is the Breast Health Clinic. We have an opening for a biopsy available next week and thought you'd like to move it up from your originally scheduled procedure. Please call our office to discuss at your earliest convenience."

Next week? That was more than a week sooner than she'd originally been told.

Anxious, Aspen checked the date of the voicemail. Yesterday.

"Please God, don't let them have filled the spot already."

She called the office back and worked her way through to the appointment desk. "Yes, this is Aspen Fairchild. I had a voicemail from yesterday about potentially being able to move up my biopsy."

"We have an opening for Monday afternoon at two."

That was literally the day after her camp session was over. She'd intended to go on and do a few other things on her list at that point, but that had all been BB—Before Brooks. Monday meant she could get answers faster. If something truly was wrong, she could get treatment faster—if there was even any-thing to be done. And if there was nothing actually wrong... she'd be free and clear to see if Brooks was interested in something more than this week. The lure of that potential future was too much to resist.

"I'll be there."

She took down all the information about time, place, and what she was expected to do. She'd need to change her flight home, but that could wait a little bit. There were other messages wait-ing, including one from Linnea.

"Girl, call me. Immediately."

Alarmed by the urgency in her friend's tone, she hit Linnea's contact. The phone rang only twice before she picked up.

"Aspen! Oh my God!"

Worry shot through her like lightning. "What? What happened? Did something happen to the shop? Are you okay?"

"I can't believe you didn't tell me!"

Her brain struggled to keep up. "What do you mean I didn't tell you? About what?"

"You and Brooks Hennessy! How the hell did that happen?"

The breath clogged in her throat. "How... how do you even know about it?"

"Girl, it's all over the internet."

She sank down onto the nearest bench. "What?"

"Yeah. People are talking about you and speculating about the two of you. It's a whole big thing. You're *engaged*?"

"No, not exactly. It's complicated." Okay, maybe this wasn't much more than was already out there. She'd known there were photos. Linnea would have recognized her.

"But you're with Brooks Hennessy?"

"Yeah, I am."

"That's gonna be a story for the ages, I feel sure. But did you not know that the press has, like, your name and everything?"

The lovely relaxation from her massage evaporated, and dread took up residence in her belly. "Oh God. No. I knew they had my photo, but I didn't know they knew who I was. Not really."

Wasn't Brooks' publicist supposed to be handling all this?

"Oh yeah, they know who you are. They know where you're from. They even know about how your mom died so suddenly."

"What? Why would they even be talking about that? It was years ago." Not that it made Aspen feel any less ill at the idea.

"Well, there's a lot of speculation that the two of you connected over grief, given how his mom died. It's a whole big thing. Everybody's trying to figure out how y'all met and how long you've been together since you came out of left field."

Aspen dropped her head into her hands. "Shit." Obviously, they had connected over grief, but that wasn't anyone's business but their own.

"I was afraid of this. That you didn't know. I felt certain I would've heard from you if you did."

It was one thing to have her face out there when nobody knew who she was. She hadn't minded being the mystery woman in his life, hadn't cared what kind of speculation might be out there. This had all begun as something temporary. But it had turned into so much more. And now the public knew who she was, knew where she was from, and clearly they were digging into her private life. Them publicly discussing her mother's death made her feel utterly violated.

"Hang on a minute."

Toggling over to a browser, she searched for her name. There'd never been much in the past on the rare occasions she'd thought to look, but she was on the front page of results now. Every single article and post connected her to Brooks. She opened a few and skimmed.

Aspen Fairchild, of Cooper's Bend, Georgia, is the mystery woman who's captured the heart of one of hockey's favorite sons...

Hockey fans are baffled how the two met...

Fairchild, who lost her mother to an aggressive form of cancer ten years ago, just might be the perfect person to help Hennessy through his own recent loss...

None of it was ugly or disrespectful, but it was private. They knew where she was from and had obviously talked to someone back home, or where would they have gotten the information about her mother? That was the thing that bothered her most. Maybe they'd mined her social media. It was a long time ago. She couldn't remember what she'd posted. But either way, they'd dug into her life. Would no doubt keep digging because they'd decided she was worthy of their attention due only to her association with Brooks.

All of this was wrong on so many levels.

"I've gotta go. I need to go talk to Brooks."

"Of course. And honey, when you can, will you *please* tell me how all of this came about?"

"I'll tell you everything as soon as I get home on Sunday."

"I thought you were going to be gone for longer."

"My procedure got moved up."

"Need me to pick you up at the airport?"

"That would be great. I'll text you my flight details as soon as I have them."

"You've got it."

"Thanks. See you in a few days."

She hung up the phone, head reeling.

How had they figured out who she was? She hadn't posted a thing on social media since she got up here. Neither had Brooks. That had been part of their staying on the down-low plan. Had someone at the camp outed them? Certainly, a lot of the staff knew who she was, at least in conjunction with Brooks. Worse... could there be reporters hiding out among the guests?

Feeling suddenly paranoid, she looked around at the other campers wandering the grounds, wondering if any of them were watching her.

Aspen shoved the phone back into her pocket.

Brooks was due to meet her back at the cabin any minute now. They'd just have to figure this out together.

Somehow.

BROOKS WAS STILL TRYING to figure out what to say by the time he made it back to the cabin. How did you tell your... whatever the hell Aspen was to him... that her whole life was now up for dissection by total strangers? That these vultures had dug up the details of her mother's death and trotted them out for all to see. And fuck, reading that had hurt him. He couldn't imagine what it had been like for her to live it.

He knew her well enough by now to understand that she was an intensely private person. There was no question she'd be upset about all of this. The real issue was how much, and whether she would blame him for all of it. Because it was his fault. Not directly. He hadn't put the information out there. But no one would have gone looking if she hadn't been involved with him. If he hadn't talked her into this lunatic fake engagement because he'd just wanted to spend more time with her. But he'd truly believed they'd have more time before anyone got curious enough to go searching this much.

Aspen turned from the window when he stepped inside. One look at her face and he knew. He *knew* she'd somehow found out. The skin around her eyes and mouth was drawn, and both arms were wrapped around her middle in a self-protective gesture.

His immediate instinct was to comfort and apologize. But on the remote chance he was wrong, he had to ask. "What's wrong? What's happened?"

"They know who I am. They know everything. Or maybe not everything, but enough. My name. Where I'm from. That I lost my mother. They're digging into my private life, Brooks."

So, their blissful little bubble had well and truly burst.

Time to face the music, Hennessy.

He closed the distance between them, cupping her elbows and drawing her into his arms. "I know. I'm sorry. So fucking sorry. I knew this was a possibility, but I didn't think they would figure it out this fast. And I had no idea they'd go into such intimate detail about your mom."

She blinked luminous green eyes at him, her face blanking. "How much detail? The article I saw only mentioned that she'd died of cancer. They were hypothesizing that was how we connected."

Oh, it was so much more than that. If she hadn't seen it yet, he sure as hell didn't want to be responsible for putting her through that.

Her hands curled into his shirt. "How much detail, Brooks?"

Knowing he couldn't lie to her, he swallowed. "Everything. Or a damned big portion of it."

"Show me."

She might as well be asking him to stab her through the heart himself. "Aspen, you don't need to see—"

"Show me," she insisted.

Reluctantly, he dropped his hold on her and found the article again on his phone, handing it over to her.

She began to read. After the first few lines, she wilted down onto the bed, her hair falling forward to curtain her face as she continued. One hand lifted to cover her mouth.

Brooks could do nothing but stand and wait, every inch of his skin itching with the need to do something to fix the unfixable. To find a way to put the genie back in the bottle. To protect her from a threat that had already gotten past his guard.

Aspen's shoulders shook by the end, and when

she lifted her head, her face was a mask of devastation, tears streaming down her cheeks. "They didn't just dig this up on social media. They talked to people at home about me. About my family. Probably the only reason I haven't heard from my dad is that he and Tricia are still out of the country. He probably hasn't seen. But someone will tell him. Because it's his life, too."

Miserable, Brooks didn't know if he should try to touch her or not. Maybe she wouldn't want his comfort now. "I'm sorry. I know that's nothing in the face of all this, but I don't know what else to say."

"What gives them the right to think they can do this?" she demanded.

"I don't know. I don't understand these people any more than you do. I can't justify anything that they've done or said."

"How can you stand it?"

"How...?" He didn't know how to answer that.

"How is it that they think they have any right to parade anyone's personal information out there for public consumption?" She shoved to her feet and began to pace. "No wonder things have been so bad for you since your mom died. They keep throwing it in your face. As if you're a story for the public's entertainment, not a person in your own right. If they did this to me, they must have done as much or worse to you."

Wait... what?

Aspen stopped in front of him, lifting a hand to his cheek. "I'm sorry. I'm so sorry that you have to deal with this. That they think that they have some claim to you." Her arms slid around him in a hug, and somehow... she was the one comforting him.

How the hell had that happened? This was all his fault. She'd been put in the crosshairs because of him, and she was still thinking of him. This woman was so kind. And that made what the press had done that much worse.

Brooks pulled her in, wiping her lingering tears with his thumb.

"Is there anything we can do to stop this?"

"Stop it?" He shook his head. "No. I've learned over the years that the media is very much a juggernaut in that sense. All we can do is to try to control the narrative. I can contact my publicist, Rebekah, to see if she has any suggestions. Maybe we can get her to make some sort of public statement requesting that everybody respect our right to privacy. But I don't know that it's going to do any good."

"It's something." On a sigh, she settled her head against his chest. "You know, it's ironic."

"What is?"

"The only thing they didn't seem to uncover is the lie. No one is questioning that we're really engaged. Wondering where and how we met? Yeah. How long we've been together? Yes. But nobody is suggesting that it isn't real."

For a long minute he was struck speechless. Not that the media hadn't uncovered their deception, but because his immediate instinct had been that it *was* real. That she was his and this thing between them was more than the lie.

As he held her in the middle of their shared cabin, Brooks wondered if there was a chance in hell of getting his wish in the face of reality.

11

"Are you okay?"

Aspen was most definitely nowhere in the vicinity of okay. But because Brooks seemed so miserable and had been essentially flagellating himself all afternoon, she tipped her head to his shoulder and lied through her teeth. "I'm fine."

The in-depth article she'd read recounting her mother's death had brought all the fear and grief she'd felt at eighteen back to the forefront. Finding out that her mother was going to die. That she wouldn't be around for Aspen's wedding or the birth of her children. That she wouldn't live to see Aspen graduate college. Wouldn't even make it to see her graduate high school. They weren't going to get any extra time. No more tomorrows. No future of any kind.

Except this time, it wasn't just the devastation of knowing she was losing the person she loved most in the world. Now Aspen was living it all as if it was happening to her. Because there was every chance that it was. That the lump she'd found was a death sentence. Over these past days with Brooks, she'd dared to have some kind of hope. To believe that maybe... just maybe... there'd be a chance for more. That she'd get a reprieve.

But the reality was that even if this lump wasn't the thing that would kill her, chances were, she'd end up with something worse later. The genetic lottery was stacked against her, and she couldn't lie to herself about it anymore. How could she possibly be selfish enough to hurt Brooks like that? How could she even consider asking him to be with her for the long term, with that risk hanging over her head? She didn't want to be someone else that he loved and lost. If he could even love her at all. And she thought that maybe, after everything they'd been through, he could love her. Eventually. It didn't feel too arrogant to believe he was developing feelings for her as she was for him.

Which meant she had a choice to make. She

could change her flight to go back on Sunday as she'd originally intended, getting home to Georgia in just enough time to make it to her biopsy on Monday. Or she could go sooner, while things were still good between them. Before she was forced to tell him the full truth.

There were no good options here. Either she hurt him with the reality of her situation, further traumatizing him in the wake of his mom's death. Or she hurt him by ghosting him and telling him nothing at all. There was no means of getting out of this situation where either of them ended up unscathed. But every day that passed, they got closer. The kindest thing to do was leave before either of them got in any deeper emotionally.

The idea of it made her physically ill.

Why had she even agreed to all this in the first place? She should've demanded her own cabin and hidden away. Except she'd been selfish. Because this trip wasn't about hiding. It was about getting out there and embracing life to the fullest. Brooks had seemed to epitomize that. He'd helped her break out of her comfort zone and really live in so many more ways than she'd anticipated.

"Respectfully, I think you're full of shit. You're not fine."

Occasionally, it was very inconvenient to be

seen. Aspen straightened. "Okay, no, I'm not." And as she pressed her brow to his, she didn't know how she ever really would be again. She couldn't imagine not waking up to him in the morning. Couldn't fathom not having him in her life. Didn't know how the hell she was going to walk away.

"I wish there was something I could do."

He'd said the same thing at least a dozen times since yesterday, and Aspen knew he'd do anything she asked. But it wasn't like she could ask him to be less wonderful or to somehow give her more strength to get through what he didn't even know was coming.

Except... maybe she could ask him for something that would get the same end result.

"You know what I would really love?"

"What?"

"Reese's Cups. There's that little service station and convenience store halfway to the next town. Boone's? Maybe you could go pick some up?"

"That's it? Some candy?"

"Eating my feelings seems kinda appealing just now. I haven't actually had them in years."

Brooks nodded once. "Mission accepted. Let's go get you some Reese's Cups." He held out his hand.

"I don't actually want to leave the cabin right

now. It feels like everybody is looking at me." Not a lie. Their foray out for lunch had made her feel as if she were under a microscope.

"Fair point. I shall brave the wilds beyond camp proper to satisfy your sweet tooth. Any second choices if they're out of Reese's?"

"Snickers is also a solid choice."

"Got it." He snagged his keys and hesitated. "Are you sure you'll be okay here by yourself?"

"Yeah. I think I might just read a little. Or have a nap."

"Okay. I'll be back. And when I am, maybe we can Netflix and chill."

Aspen arched a brow. "In which sense? The euphemistic kind or the literal?"

"Whichever your heart desires."

She forced a smile and hoped he didn't see the strain around the edges. "That's a plan."

He bent to brush a kiss over her lips, and Aspen couldn't quite stop herself from framing his face and lingering just a few moments, doing her best to commit the taste and feel of him to memory.

"Thank you," she whispered.

His smile was just a little crooked. "Anything for you."

Then he was gone, trotting down the front steps and headed toward the parking lot.

Aspen waited until he was out of sight before hauling her suitcase out from under the bed. Her hands shook as she yanked open drawers, gathering up clothes and dumping them into the bag. She had to hurry. Had to get out of here before he got back because if she saw him again, she'd never actually be able to leave. And she had to leave. It was what was best for him.

In less than fifteen minutes she was packed. She made a call to the lodge to ask about transportation to the train station in Briarsted, explaining that she had an emergency and needed to leave early. A staff member would be waiting at the parking lot in ten minutes. After she hung up, she made one last sweep of the cabin to make sure she'd gotten everything.

At the door, she hesitated.

This was the right thing. It had to be.

Taking a firmer grip on her bag, she headed for the parking lot.

IT TOOK LONGER than Brooks wanted to find Reese's Cups. Boone's had been out, so he'd trekked all the way to Briarsted to find somewhere still open that had some. The dozen packs he'd bought were probably more than she'd be able to eat in one go, but he'd wanted so desperately to do something—anything—to make her feel better. Because he knew exactly what it felt like to have a private grief splashed about for public consumption. That had been his life for the past several months. Understanding the desire to cocoon, he'd also bought popcorn and wine, in case she preferred to spend the remainder of their trip caved up in the cabin.

Hell, maybe he ought to look into booking them somewhere else. Somewhere truly out of the public eye. There was bound to be somewhere she'd want to go where nobody knew who either of them was. He was running through the options in his head as he carried his snack stash back to the cabin from the parking lot. The best options were out of the country. Maybe some tropical island or a country where hockey wasn't even a sport. Did she have a passport? It wasn't like his was on him, so it would require a trip back to Denver to pick it up. Unless he could get Colter or Grady to overnight it...

He trotted up the stairs and into the cabin. "Hey, Aspen, how do you feel about leaving the country?"

No answer.

At a glance, he could see the bathroom door was open.

Maybe she'd gotten stir crazy and decided to go for a run.

Except... Brooks didn't see her e-reader on the nightstand. And her extra shoes weren't lined up by the wall. Dropping his groceries on the bed, he checked the bathroom.

The counter was clear of her toiletries.

With a sick, sinking feeling, he dropped to one knee to check under the bed.

Her suitcase was gone.

"No. No, no, no, no, no."

He'd thought they were okay. He'd believed they were in this together. Surely... *Surely,* she didn't leave. Not again.

But what other explanation could there be?

She had no transportation. She hadn't driven up here as he had, she'd ridden the camp bus from New York. So maybe she hadn't actually managed to get off the property.

Yanking open the door, he started to bolt down the path, only to run into Heather Tully, the blonde who'd checked him in at the beginning of the week.

"Mr. Hennessy, I have something for you." Her

usually cheerful expression was worried as she extended an envelope.

His question of whether she'd seen Aspen died on his lips as he saw his name scrawled in her handwriting across the front. Numb, he mumbled, "Thanks," and sank down on the top step to read.

Dear Brooks,

I know you're angry right now. You have every right to be. I almost didn't leave this note, but that would have been too much like really ghosting you, and you're too important to me to hurt like that. The truth is that I had to go. We were both getting in too deep, too far in over our heads. And the fact of the matter is that I've been keeping something from you.

You know that my mother died of a very aggressive form of breast cancer. There is every chance that I am in the same boat. Right before I planned this trip, I found a lump. That was what precipitated this whole thing, because I realized that I hadn't been living the life that I was given. I know better than almost anyone how quickly that can be ripped away. The idea that this is the only time that I'd get propelled me out of my comfort zone and my personal bubble to do all of these wonderful things.

It brought me to you.

I never set out to use you. I never set out to hurt you. And I told myself that it would be okay because it was just for this week. Then we'd separate, and you'd go on your merry way, never having to know if anything bad happened to me. But I know you better now, and I don't think I was alone in feeling like this could have gone somewhere.

Brooks, I can't put you through that. I can't hurt you that way.

I never planned to tell you any of this. I know this is going to hurt you. But knowing how devastated you were by the fact that your mom didn't even tell you that she was sick, I couldn't do the same. You deserve to know the reason.

I wish beyond anything you can imagine that things were different. That we could have had that chance. But I'm never so lucky, and you deserve better from someone who will be around for all the tomorrows.

Please know that these have been the best days of my life, and you are the best man I know.

Always,

Aspen

The bottom dropped out of Brooks' world. If he hadn't already been sitting, he'd have fallen to his knees.

Cancer. She was saying she had cancer. Or thought she did. And she'd run from him trying to protect him because she might be dying.

But it was too fucking late. He already loved

her. That was what this brutal, tearing grief he felt meant. He loved her, and he hadn't gotten the chance to tell her.

"Fuck this shit."

He reached for his phone, determined to track her down. To talk about all of this. But he realized he still hadn't gotten her contact information. It hadn't been necessary because they'd been together almost every waking minute since they'd arrived at Camp Firefly Falls.

If Aspen was already gone—and since Heather had brought him this letter, chances were good that she was—he had absolutely no way to reach her.

She was alone. Maybe dying. And he couldn't get to her. He buried his face in his hands.

"Hey, are you okay?"

Brooks looked up to find one of the women from the archery range standing on the path running past the cabin, looking concerned. "I... no."

"Do you want me to go find your fiancée for you?"

His heart seized. "You can't. She's gone."

"Gone?" She blinked in surprise. "Oh, Brooks, I'm so sorry."

Confused, he looked back at her just in time to

see her phone aimed in his direction, capturing his devastation for all to see.

12

Aspen woke in her childhood bedroom feeling as if she'd been hit by a truck. A glance at the clock told her she'd been down for nearly twelve hours, partly from pure exhaustion, partly from grief. It had been past midnight by the time she'd landed in Atlanta, and even later when the Uber dropped her home all the way back in Cooper's Bend. Given the hour and the short notice, she hadn't even texted Linnea she was coming home until she'd walked through the front door.

She rolled out of bed and stumbled downstairs for water, guzzling a full glass while standing at the fridge. Dehydration was a thing. Though the prospect of food wasn't remotely appealing, she opened the fridge and pantry to check her options. Other than condiments and a single, lonely egg, there was next to nothing. She wasn't particularly keen on the canned chili she found hanging out on a shelf. Her dad had already moved most of his stuff down to Savannah, and Aspen hadn't bothered stocking things before her own trip. Hell, the house was still full of all the boxes of her stuff she hadn't taken the time to unpack before hitting the road. She'd had just enough time to empty her apartment.

The prospect of getting out for groceries made her want to curl up and hide. She'd spent the whole frantic trip home trying to make herself invisible, lest someone recognize her from the photos circulating online. The baseball cap and total lack of makeup—she'd cried all of it off—had probably helped with that. But she wouldn't be so lucky at home. Would reporters be lurking somewhere? Worse, what if she ran into the locals who'd been running their mouths about her? There'd be questions. Lots of questions. Probably at the top of the list would be, "Where is Brooks?"

That wasn't a question she was up to answering yet.

She'd known walking away from him would hurt. But God, she hadn't anticipated the visceral ache of knowing things between them were over. And they were over. Telling him the truth had made sure of that. It didn't matter that deep down, she knew she'd done the right thing for him. The loss cut deep.

The doorbell rang.

Aspen flinched, wondering who it was. A reporter who'd tracked down her home? Her dad? A neighbor who'd seen her come back late last night?

For a moment, she considered ignoring it, but the bell sounded again, followed by a pounding on the door. Someone knew she was here and wasn't going away until she answered.

Bracing herself for whatever—or whoever—was on the other side, she went to answer.

Linnea stood on the front stoop, to-go cups in hand.

"What are you doing here? Shouldn't you be at the coffee shop?"

She pushed inside. "The coffee shop is covered. Where do you think I'm going to be when you text me in the middle of the damn night to say that you've already hurried home and that you're at the house? What the actual hell? Here." She shoved one of the cups into Aspen's hand.

The familiar scent of her favorite pomegranate

green tea wafted up. It was a kindness Aspen hadn't expected and didn't feel like she deserved, and she promptly burst into tears.

Linnea instantly wrapped her in a hug. "Oh, honey. Tell me everything."

So Aspen did. Over the course of two cups of tea—both of them had been for her—she spilled the whole damned story out, from her impromptu rescue of him at the hotel bar, all the way through to the subterfuge she'd used to get him out of the way long enough for her to run.

When she'd finished, Linnea leaned back on the sofa, studying her. "You love him."

"Yeah, I do." No point in denying it here. "That's why this hurts so damned much."

"And you just walked away."

"I had to."

"Bullshit." Though Linnea's tone was mild, Aspen flinched.

"Didn't you hear anything I said about how he lost his mom? It really fucked him up. He doesn't need to be in a relationship with somebody else who has cancer."

"You don't know that you have cancer. You have Schrödinger's Boob. You know, like that cat thing from our gen psych class back in college. Right now you are in a stage where you don't know. You have one reality in which you have some form of cancer. In the other reality, there is a completely benign reason for your lump. You're making assumptions about which reality you exist in and making decisions based on that information that, frankly, is questionable. You threw away something really great because you're afraid."

Aspen shook her head. "It's not just that—although, yes, I'm afraid. I'm fucking terrified. But I cannot hurt him like that."

Linnea laid a hand on her knee. "Honey, I think your heart is in the right place. And it's admirable that you don't want to hurt him. But what do you think your leaving just did?"

"It was the lesser of all evils. There was no scenario in which he wasn't hurt at all. But I had to get out before we got in any deeper. Before he fell for me."

Her friend arched a disbelieving eyebrow. "Honey, it is way too late for that. Have you looked at any of the pictures of you two?"

"What are you talking about?"

Linnea grabbed her phone, tapping and swiping for a few seconds before handing it over. There was an array of photos beyond just the Empire State Building. Several shots had been taken of them at Camp Firefly Falls. And in every single

one they looked like exactly what they'd pur-
ported to be—a happily in love engaged couple.

Tears slid down her cheeks again.

"He clearly feels the same," Linnea said gently.
"It seems a shame to let that go."

Aspen wavered. "Maybe I can contact him
again after I get the results of my biopsy. After I
know that it's safe. But I don't know that he'll want
to talk to me again."

"He's gonna want to talk to you again. He's
probably losing his damn mind with you not
being there."

"Maybe not. I left him a letter explaining
everything. It seemed more cruel not to do that."

Linnea seemed to choose her words very carefully. "I'm sure he's upset. But if he's the kind of
guy who will consider what you did a good thing
and a bullet dodged, then he's not worthy of your
time or affections. If he is, instead, as heart-
broken as you are, then it only makes sense to try
to win him back." She straightened. "You need
food. I'm sure you don't have a lick of it in the
house. I'm Door Dashing some lunch. You go
grab a shower, then we're gonna sit down and
figure out a plan."

"I cannot go back to him if I truly have cancer.
I'm simply not going to do that to him. I refuse. I'm

not going to be somebody else that he cares about and loses. He deserves better than that."

Though Linnea looked a little like she wanted to throttle her, she didn't argue. "Okay, fine. We will make a contingency plan for the circumstance under which Schrödinger's Boob is fine."

"I can live with that."

"Go shower off all your travels. You'll feel better."

Aspen did as she was told, and she did feel better with clean hair and clean clothes.

The doorbell was ringing again as she got downstairs, so she opened it to find Rita Timmons, one of the Blue-Hair Mafia who were the town busybodies. She and her posse had taken up Door Dash as a means of seeing people in their retirement and in hopes of getting the scoop on the latest gossip.

Rita looked Aspen up and down in such a way that it made her glad she'd just cleaned up. As she offered up the bag with the food, she clucked her tongue. "How dare you break that young man's heart?"

"Excuse me?"

But Rita didn't bother replying before turning on her sneakered heel and striding away.

"What the hell was that about?" Linnea asked.

"I don't know, but I have a bad feeling about it."

Carrying the food back to the kitchen, Aspen set it down and pulled out her phone to do a quick Google search for "Brooks Hennessy engagement."

The very first result brought up a photo of Brooks' face, looking utterly devastated. The headline? *Trouble in Paradise for Hennessy and His Honey?*

"Oh God."

Aspen skimmed more articles with similar headlines, all discussing his heartbreak and painting her in the worst possible light.

"How the hell did the media already get wind of this? It's been less than 24 hours." Unless... Brooks told them himself.

She toggled back to the photo. It had been taken on the steps of their cabin, and he looked utterly blindsided. By her defection, or by whoever had snapped the picture?

Linnea snatched the phone from her hand. "Okay, that's enough of that. You are officially banned from social media and the Internet for awhile, until all of this dies down. You have one focus and one focus alone, and that is your biopsy and doing whatever is necessary to see that you are healthy."

Aspen swallowed back the fresh tears that wanted to fall. "Okay."

"And we'll cross the bridge of everything else after you have an answer and go from there."

And because there was nothing else she could do, Aspen did as she was told.

"Do you think it will work?"

Brooks was only half listening to Rebekah's reply as he followed the GPS directions from his dash.

"I mean, I don't know. I don't think it'll stop everything, but it can't hurt. Are you sure you want to do this?"

"The press is eviscerating her over something that isn't her fault. Yes, I want to put out a press release taking full blame for everything." It wasn't precisely accurate—their situation was too complicated to lay blame at only one door—but he'd gladly take a knee to protect her from the vipers in the media.

"Okay. I'll reach out to my media connections and send it out."

"Thanks, Rebekah. I gotta go. I think I'm almost there."

"Good luck. I hope this goes the way you want it to."

"Me, too."

Brooks hung up and made the final turn onto a tree-lined street in Cooper's Bend, Georgia. He had no idea whether the public statement he'd issued, taking all the fault for the dissolution of their relationship, would actually do a damned thing. But he'd had to do something. God willing, Aspen hadn't seen any of that coverage.

He really hoped she hadn't. She didn't need that kind of negativity in her condition.

"Your destination is on the right."

He pulled his G-Wagon to the curb and looked at the neat brick duplex nestled back amid some trees. The attached garage was closed, so he couldn't see if there was a vehicle home. Rubbing his palms on his jeans, he braced himself. It felt more than a little stalkerish just showing up at her place, but if there was one bonus to the invasive search of the press, it had been in helping track down exactly where he needed to go to win Aspen back. He'd driven the sixteen hours from Camp Firefly Falls, all the way to Aspen's hometown with only a handful of stops and not nearly enough sleep.

Jittery from all the coffee and energy drinks

that had fueled his mission, he slid out of the driver's seat and strode up the walk, knocking on her door.

No one answered.

Maybe she was hiding inside.

Brooks knocked again, harder this time. "Aspen! It's me. Please open up."

The door to the other half of the duplex opened, and some guy stuck his head out. "You looking for Aspen?"

"Yeah."

"She doesn't live there anymore. She moved out."

What the actual fuck? Were things so bad that she'd moved the moment she got home?

He scrubbed a hand over his face. "Do you know where she went?"

"Sorry, man. No."

"Thanks."

It was only as he slid back into his SUV that he remembered Aspen's father had gifted her the house she'd grown up in. Maybe she'd gone there. Except, he had no idea where that was. It seemed to be the one piece the media *hadn't* dug up, whether because they hadn't thought to look, or because that was where the locals drew the line in violating her privacy. But there had to be someone here who both knew where she was and would be willing to tell him.

Opening up social media, Brooks scrolled to her profile. There wasn't a lot on there. As he'd known, Aspen was a pretty private person. But there were quite a few pictures she'd been tagged in by someone named Linnea Barton. Clicking the link, he browsed her profile. Linnea was a lot more public, evidently because she owned the local coffee shop, The Sword and the Scone. That was as good a place as any to try next.

Plugging the address into his GPS, he set out for downtown Cooper's Bend.

The town itself was cute, if a little run down. The sort of place that was probably one sneeze away from a revival if the right person took the helm. Settled along the banks of a river, the downtown had historic appeal mixed with the sort of heavily timber-based architecture that was common in mountain towns. He found a parking space and circled back on Cohutta Street toward The Sword and the Scone.

Brooks didn't know exactly what he'd expected from the name, but stepping into something that felt like the set of a Renaissance Faire hadn't quite been it. Under other circumstances, he'd have been amused by the commitment to the theme.

Right now, his only concern was finding Linnea Barton and prying Aspen's location out of her.

He didn't spot his quarry behind the counter. Not ready to give up, he joined the early lunch line that was already half-a-dozen deep, and snaking back toward the door. He did his best to be patient and not cut in front of all the other waiting patrons, though every instinct was shouting that he needed to hurry.

Abruptly, the older black woman working the register looked past the customer she was ringing up and spotted him. There was zero question from the look on her face that she'd recognized him. As she stared, everyone else waiting turned around and looked, clearly curious.

"I'll get that order ready for you in just a minute, sugar. Excuse me for a sec." The woman scooted out from behind the counter and made straight for him.

"Brooks?"

"Yes."

She snagged him by the arm and began towing him back toward the door. Oh hell, was he about to be thrown out? "I'm not here to cause trouble. I just need to find Linnea Barton."

Instead of dragging him outside, the woman tugged him into one of the alcoves of tables.

"Linnea isn't here. But that's not really who you're looking for, is it?"

"No. I'm trying to find Aspen Fairchild. But you knew that already, didn't you?"

"Mmmhmm." The woman crossed her arms, and Brooks could practically see the walls going up. This would be the dragon protecting her charge. Fitting, given the name of the coffeeshop. "What are you doing here?"

"I came to talk to her."

"Talk? Really?"

Brooks didn't want to get into their personal shit with a stranger. But he had a feeling that if he didn't give her something, he wasn't going to get anywhere. "She didn't give me a chance. She made a decision for me about the state of our relationship, and I'm not okay with that. I don't want to hurt her. I just want to have a conversation."

From the front of the line, the guy who'd been the last to order called out, "Hey Adojah, can you hurry it on up? I've got somewhere to be."

"Hush your mouth, Peter. This is more important." Adojah's deep, dark eyes studied him. "Do you love her?"

"Yes." No hesitation. He'd had plenty of hours of driving to come to terms with that. "I know she's going through some shit. I'm not going to let her go through it alone."

Brooks knew by the relaxing of her face that this had been the right answer.

"Good. That girl's been through enjoy in her life. She needs a good man. But she's not here. Not even in town. Linnea took her for surgery this afternoon. If you hurry, you should be able to catch her before she goes in for the procedure."

Surgery. Shit.

"Tell me where."

Adojah gave him the information, down to the address of the surgery center.

Brooks squeezed her shoulder. "Thanks."

She put a hand on his arm, stilling him. "Don't disappoint me, boy. If you hurt her, there's a boatload of people here who'll be ready to kick your behind, professional athlete or not."

"Understood."

"Take care of her."

"I intend to."

Then he took off at a dead run to get to his vehicle.

13

The surgery center waiting room was freezing. Aspen huddled in her chair, one hand tightly clasping Linnea's, and wondered how much longer it would be before they called her back. She had nothing to distract her from the rampant anxiety. Linnea had taken her phone again after she'd gone down the rabbit hole, reading more of the scathing articles calling her a shameless heartbreaker.

Despite her best friend's presence, Aspen felt achingly alone and so very afraid. Though her father was back from his honeymoon, she hadn't told him about any of this. Evidently, he'd remained in his blissful newlywed bubble and hadn't heard a thing about her "engagement." She didn't want to ruin that unless absolutely necessary, so she'd wait until she had something confirmed to tell him.

Had her mother felt fear like this? Probably not. She'd gone in for a checkup and come out with cancer. Everything had happened so fast. She hadn't had years of anticipatory fear building up. And maybe that was a kindness of a sort, because this level of worry was absolutely paralyzing.

Aspen wondered what her mom would say if she were here. She'd probably crack boob jokes and then tell Aspen what an idiot she was to let Brooks go.

I know what it is to be devastated, Mom. I just couldn't ask that of him.

But she remembered some of the appointments with her mom's oncologist, seeing her parents holding hands in the waiting room, her dad being a rock, even though he'd been absolutely breaking inside. That was love of the highest form. And Aspen felt privileged to have witnessed it, even if it had been cut off too soon. A part of her envied that love and wished she had it herself, because everyone deserved that level of dedication. Not that she wasn't grateful beyond words that Linnea was here with her. But it wasn't quite the same.

Why the hell couldn't things have been different? Why couldn't she have just been a normal woman, meeting a great guy?

Well, because without all this terror, you never would have gotten out of your comfort zone to meet him in the first place.

The truth of that almost made her cringe. Cancer seemed a really high price to pay for that kind of kick in the ass. Despite all of Linnea's talk about Schrödinger's Boob, Aspen didn't really think she'd be so lucky.

And that just brought her brain back around to the gut-churning fear. Damn it.

Some sort of commotion sounded from the lobby. A door got yanked open so hard it banged into the wall. Someone literally ran in, colliding with the front desk.

"Sir, you have to calm down."

"Aspen Fairchild," he gasped. "I'm looking for Aspen Fairchild."

Her head jerked toward that voice, and she stared.

Impossible. It can't be him.

Except she knew that blond hair, knew those shoulders and those long legs.

"Brooks?" She barely managed to choke the word out past the knot of emotion in her throat.

He swung toward her. His hair stood on end and his jaw was heavily stubbled, but his eyes—those beautiful blue eyes—lit at the sight of her. He rushed toward her, and Aspen found herself coming to her feet. Then his arms were around her, squeezing her so tight she could barely breathe. She fisted her hands in his T-shirt, closing her eyes as he swayed her because he was warm and real and *here*. The knowledge of that had tears burning her eyes.

"What..." Because her throat was constricted, she had to try again. "What are you doing here? I don't understand... *how* are you here?"

He pulled back only far enough to look into her face, frowning when he spotted the tears. One big hand reached up to brush away the handful of tears that dared to escape. "I used the press to track you to Cooper's Bend. But the address was apparently your old one. So then I ended up at the local coffeeshop, where some lady named Adojah threatened to kick my ass if I hurt you. But she told me where you were. So I'm here, because you are not gonna fucking go through this alone."

"But I—"

Brooks cut her off. "I appreciate you trying to save me from losing somebody else I love, but it's already too late. I don't want to lose you. Not now.

Not ever. And I don't care if we have three weeks or three years or a lifetime. I'm not walking away."

Aspen trembled. "That's a really lovely, noble sentiment, but I can't ask you to—"

"You're not asking. I'm telling. I love you. And I would rather have this time with you, however much we have, than leave things where they were."

There was no holding back the flood now. An ocean seemed to be pouring out of her eyes, and she hung on. What had she done to deserve this man? How had she found him in all the wide world?

For one crazy moment, she wondered if her mom and his had been in cahoots to matchmake from the afterlife. Aspen didn't know and didn't care. He was her own personal miracle because he was here, and he loved her and wanted to be here with her, no matter what.

"Um... Aspen Fairchild?"

She looked past Brooks's shoulder to see a nurse waiting to take her back. Struggling to pull herself together, she let him go and wiped at her face. "Looks like it's time." She glanced back to find Linnea and Brooks exchanging a look.

"You go with her," Linnea said. "I'm gonna wait out here."

"Are you sure?" Aspen asked.

"One thousand percent." She handed Aspen's bag over to Brooks.

He held out a hand. "Ready?"

She curled her fingers in his. "Not even a little bit. But I'm really glad you're here."

They followed the nurse back to the prep area. "You're going to want to change out of your clothes and into the hospital gown. Put your stuff in a bag here. Your..." she glanced at Brooks, clearly wondering how to refer to him.

"Fiancé," he filled in.

"Right. Your fiancé can hang onto all that while you're in surgery. He'll get paged when you come back out for recovery and will be here when you wake up." The nurse went over a few more details. "Doc is running on time today, so he should be back to get you in about half an hour."

Then she was gone, and they were alone in the little partitioned room.

Aspen arched a brow. "Fiancé?"

"We'll talk about it on the other side."

Her heart began to thump from something other than fear. "Are you sure you want to do this?"

He lifted her hand to his lips for a kiss. "I've never been more sure of anything in my life."

With that assurance ringing in her ears, she

changed into the hospital gown and slipped onto the waiting bed. Brooks held her hand, giving her all that love and support she'd seen between her parents. So when the nurses showed back up, saying it was time, she wasn't as afraid because he'd given her something to really live for.

Before they wheeled her away, he kissed her hand one more time. "I'll be here when you wake up."

"See you on the other side. And Brooks?"

"Yeah, baby?"

"I love you, too."

THE DAY after Aspen's biopsy, Brooks sat with her in a patient room at her oncologist's office, waiting for the doctor to come discuss the results. Her hand gripped his like a vise, and he knew she was scared to death. Of course she was. He was pretty damned terrified himself of what this was going to mean for her. For both of them.

They hadn't talked about any of that last night when he'd driven her home after the procedure. She'd been groggy from the anesthesia and had napped much of the evening. While she'd rested, he'd been making plans. For his career. For his life.

Because he'd been coasting long enough. Not that he'd told her any of it yet. He wanted to give her certainty, not more questions.

He wanted to give her everything.

"You don't have to be here for this," she murmured. "You don't have to go through this."

Covering their joined hands with his free one, Brooks squeezed tighter. "What can I do to make you understand I'm gonna stick?" He had some ideas, but he was saving those until they got to the other side of this.

"It's not that I don't believe you will. I know you will. And it's not that I don't want you here, or that I don't love you. I just—"

"Aspen, I know." He brushed a kiss to her brow. It meant so much that she wanted to save him pain. But it would hurt so much more to think of her going through all of this on her own. "Stop trying to give me an out. I won't take it."

The door opened, and the doctor came in. An older black man with gray at his temples, he nodded a greeting to them both as he drew up the stool and sat.

"I know that you're very anxious about all of this, especially with your mother's history, so I'm going to get straight to it." He set her chart aside. "So, there's good news and there's bad news."

"Bad news first." Her body was ramrod straight.

"You have ductal carcinoma in situ." He explained what the condition was in a lot of complicated medical jargon Brooks didn't quite follow.

"Um... layman's terms?" he asked.

"It is technically cancer, but it is effectively the pre-est form of pre-cancer that it can possibly be. We caught it very, very early. So that's good." He shifted his focus back to Aspen. "We'll go in and remove the duct, and you'll do a round of radiation to take care of any lingering cancerous cells, and that should be it. Even with your mother's history."

"But... can it spread?" Her voice wavered, and Brooks could feel her trembling through their tightly linked hands.

"The chances of it spreading or recurring are incredibly small. I mean, nobody wants cancer, but if you're gonna have cancer, this is the one to have, and this is the point to find it."

She closed her eyes and pressed a hand to her mouth, clearly overcome.

Brooks couldn't hold back any more. "So, she's going to live?"

The doctor smiled. "I have absolutely no

reason to believe that she's not going to live a long and happy life."

Aspen's breath exploded out of her, and she bent to put her head between her knees.

Relief had his own head spinning, his limbs going weak. He'd only just found her, and he wasn't going to lose her. He was going to have a chance for a life with her. And by damn, he intended to embrace all of those tomorrows.

By the time they'd made it outside, the sun seemed just a little brighter, the flowers more vibrant. Aspen had said little as the doctor went over the treatment plan and scheduled the removal of the problematic duct. She stopped at the edge of the parking lot and seemed to stare into space.

"Are you okay? How do you feel?"

She turned to face him. "I don't even know. I mean, relieved, clearly. I don't think it's real yet. I've been convinced from the moment I found the thing that I was going to be just like my mother. The possibility that it was something that's, well, obviously not benign, but relatively benign under the circumstances, didn't occur to me. So this is incredible. And I don't know what to do now."

Brooks took her hands. "I do. I think we should get married."

Aspen blinked up at him and laughed. "What?"

"I think we should get married."

The smile turned a little baffled. "Brooks, I know we were gonna talk about this whole fiancé thing, but—"

He shook his head. "No, I don't want you to be my fiancée. I want you to be my wife. I think we should live. We've both waited long enough. We can grab a flight to Vegas or drive up to Tennessee. They don't have any waiting laws there."

"How do you even know that?"

"I googled it from my phone."

"When? You haven't had your phone out since we went in there. Not since we found out."

He shrugged. "Yeah. I mean, it was my plan one way or the other. I told you. I want the time with you, whether it's three weeks or fifty years. I'd rather have the fifty years, if it's all the same to you." Her cheek was warm and smooth beneath his fingers. "I love you, Aspen. I know this is fast, and I know there's been a lot of emotional upheaval around all of this. But that hasn't changed. That's not going to change. So please, will you marry me?"

Tears welled in those gorgeous green eyes, but

he understood instinctively that this time they were happy ones. "Yeah."

Brooks whooped and scooped her up for a fast spin before setting her on her feet and taking her mouth in a dizzying, delicious kiss that was full of promises.

When at last he pulled away, he began tugging her toward the car. "The Tennessee state line isn't that far. Let's go."

Laughing again, she dragged her feet. "What? Now?"

He looked down at her with love and a teasing smirk. "Well, you've already pulled a runner on me twice, so I'm motivated to lock this down."

Color bloomed in her cheeks, but her eyes sparkled. "Fair enough. But we have some calls to make first."

EPILOGUE

"Honey, are you sure you wanna do this? I mean, this is awfully fast."

Aspen stopped fussing with the skirt on her wedding dress and folded her hands around her dad's arm. "I know. But sometimes you just know. You and mom did. And I spent most of the last ten years not keeping the promise mom asked of me. I put everything off out of fear and was too afraid to really *live*. And I'm not doing that anymore. Especially now."

She'd finally told her dad about the cancer and her prognosis in the same conversation she'd admitted she was eloping. His head was still spinning, but he and Tricia and her step-siblings Heidi and Everett had shown up for the wedding anyway. Aspen had to admit, after all the years of being just the two of them, it was lovely to have more family.

"Everything should be fine. And hopefully, everything will stay fine for the rest of my life. But in case it doesn't, I want to have lived. I love Brooks, and he loves me."

His hand covered hers and squeezed. "That's the only thing I really care about. If you're happy."

"I am."

"Then I will make every effort to like him."

Aspen snorted. "Dad!"

"What? You're my only daughter. I'm entitled."

"Fair enough."

"He'd better take good care of you."

She thought of everything he'd done since they'd met. Especially since he'd come to Georgia. "He takes excellent care of me."

"What are y'all gonna do? I mean, for everything else? Where will you live? He's a hockey player, right? Who does he even play for?" It said a lot about how fast all of this had happened that her father still didn't know about all the media coverage they'd had of their "engagement." She wasn't the only one who wasn't into sportsball.

She didn't actually know the answer to his question. They hadn't discussed any of that. Not whether he was retiring or whether he'd be going back to the ColoradoAvalanche for pre-season in a few months. Brooks had declared that could all wait until after the wedding and her surgery.

"We'll figure it out." For all that she was a planner and preferred to think of All The Things in advance, she'd decided to just roll with this. It wasn't worth putting life off anymore to figure out all the details. She was confident they would make it work. Because having this chance was worth it.

"Miss Fairchild?" The venue wedding planner stuck her head in the door of the suite. "It's time."

Aspen's heart fluttered as she grabbed up her bouquet of mountain flowers. She was really doing this. She was marrying the man she loved. And from somewhere in the back of her mind, she could hear her mother's joyful laugh.

Good job, kid.

She and her dad followed the wedding planner outside. The venue was teeny, with rows of small benches flanking a short aisle leading up to an arbor built at the edge of the deck over-looking the Great Smoky Mountains. Their handful of guests were already seated. Tricia and her two kids. Linnea. And on Brooks's side, his friends Grady and Colter, whom she'd met when they'd arrived last night from Denver.

Brooks stood at the altar, looking utterly mouthwatering in a tux. As he spotted her, his smile spread wide. Aspen felt an echoing grin split her face as the music began, and her father escorted her down the short aisle and handed her over to her husband to be.

Brooks squeezed her hands and whispered, "You look incredible."

"So do you." And she was already thinking about what it would be like to peel off the layers of that monkey suit when she got him alone later.

Their officiant beamed at the assembly. "Dearly beloved..."

The ceremony was short and sweet and absolutely perfect because it didn't make them wait to start their new lives together any longer than absolutely necessary.

"You may kiss the bride."

Brooks tipped her back in a dramatic dip that had her laughing as he took her mouth to much enthusiastic applause and cheering from their handful of guests. They'd done it! They were married! Holy crap.

They practically danced back down the aisle and into the lodge for the cake and cocktails reception.

He pulled her aside into an alcove. "I've got something to give you."

She arched a brow. "Oh?"

"A wedding present."

"I mean, I'm very excited for that, but we might require a little more privacy..."

He grinned. "Not that. But definitely that. All of that later. This is an actual present."

Aspen sobered. "I don't have yours with me."

"That's totally fine. But I didn't want to wait to give you this." Reaching into his jacket, he pulled out an envelope.

Confused, she took it, opening the flap and pulling out the stack of papers inside. It was some sort of contract. "I don't understand. What is this?"

"I didn't want to mention it unless I could pull it off, but everything's finalized. I've just been transferred to Atlanta."

Aspen frowned. "Atlanta doesn't have a hockey team."

"It does now. They're starting a new one. The Firebirds. I'm part of the initial roster, so I'll be based in Atlanta—only a little over an hour away. I'll be able to commute in for practice, so you don't have to leave Cooper's Bend unless you want to. I mean, I'd love to have you on the road with me for away games, but I know you can't leave your shop."

"What do you mean? I don't have a physical storefront. My shop is online. There's absolutely no reason I can't come with you on the road."

"Really?"

"Yeah."

On another whoop of excitement, he scooped her up and swung her in a circle. Laughing, she wrapped her arms around his shoulders. "Well, I guess I'm going to have to break my lifelong streak of ignoring sportsball and actually learn about hockey."

"Only if you want to, wife of mine."

"I find myself very motivated."

FROM HER POSITION in the stands, Aspen tried to follow the fast-paced action on the ice. Still new to the intricacies of hockey, even after attending every single one of Brooks' games this season, home and away, she frequently only managed to follow her husband. She'd had no idea when he'd taken her to the rink last summer that he could move like this. No matter what else was going on during the game, she loved watching him skate.

He was all grace and muscular control, and now she understood everything that went into honing that athlete's body she loved so much.

Her phone vibrated with a series of texts, and she tugged it out to find a message in the family group chat.

> Dad: This one's a nail biter. No score this late into the third period?

> Everett: Brooks is really moving out there.

> Heidi: Can he introduce me to Niko Petrov?

Aspen snorted and texted back.

> Aspen: The goalie is too old for you.

> Tricia: They're all too old for her!

> Heidi: I'm nearly twenty!

Tricia: GIF of woman with fingers in her ears singing la la la la la.

From the ice there was a cacophony of sounds —the clash of sticks, the scraping of skates—and then a sudden roar from the crowd.

Aspen's head snapped up, scanning for the source of the action. A flurry of activity around the opposing team's goal caught her attention, and suddenly Brooks emerged in a flash of orange and white with the puck at his stick. As he approached the goal, he made a sharp feint to the left, prompting the goalie to shift. With a flick of his wrist, he shot the puck, deftly shooting for the now-exposed corner of the net. Aspen almost missed the moment the puck hit the back of the net, the motion was so swift and seamless.

Aspen shot to her feet as the crowd erupted in a tidal wave of cheers and applause. Brooks caught her eye as he skated by. His chest heaved, his face sheened with sweat, but his blue eyes sparked with the thrill of scoring. Grinning, she blew him a kiss. Aware of the curious glances around her, she announced, "That's my husband!" Not that she was being subtle about it. Every game she showed up in a custom jersey with his number that read MRS. HENNESSY on the back.

As was his habit, Brooks blew a kiss back before resuming his focus on the game.

This was the last game of the season, and Atlanta had done remarkably well for being a new team. She'd learned to enjoy the game and had traveled all over with him during the season, but she was ready to have him to herself for a bit. Between the surgery and treatment and the start of the season, they hadn't had time for a proper honeymoon. But all of it was worth it because she'd been officially declared cancer free.

Since last summer, they'd been making a list for all the things she wanted to do. As they'd been able, on breaks and when the occasion arose while they traveled the country for away games, Brooks had helped her check quite a few off. She'd seen Niagara Falls. Walked Rodeo Drive. Swum with dolphins in Florida. And she'd learned to skate more than passably well—even if she did periodically fake a stumble just to have Brooks save her all over again. With his ring on her finger, she figured she was entitled.

Now they'd be setting off next week for two whole months of globetrotting between seasons, while they worked their way through sixteen countries and three continents. Aspen couldn't wait.

When the final buzzer sounded, Atlanta was up 1–0 and the crowd went wild. Used to the post-game chaos now, Aspen patiently made her way from her rink-side seat to the area where the press usually paused to interview players fresh from the game. She spotted a female reporter interviewing Brooks.

"—yet again, you score the winning goal. To what do you credit your success?"

He spotted her at the periphery and reached out to snag her, pulling her into the frame. "I've got my good luck charm." He gave her a smacking kiss.

Aspen's cheeks heated and she ducked her gaze, even as a satisfied smile curved her lips. After nine months of marriage, she still wasn't quite used to being so frequently in the public eye. But since they'd been declared one of hockey's most adorable couples, at least the attention had been mostly positive. She even occasionally got asked for *her* autograph.

"Are you disappointed not to make the playoffs this year?"

Brooks tucked her against his side, his big hand curved possessively around her hip as he answered. "No, I'm not disappointed at all. We've spent this season really building the team, working to create cohesion. We've been successful at that, so everybody better look out next season because the Firebirds are going to be a force to be reckoned with."

The reporter smiled. "What do you plan to do next?"

His grin was impish. "I'm planning to take my wife on a new adventure."

"Congratulations, you two."

With a little wave, they turned away from the camera.

"There you have it, folks." Behind them, the commentator continued to make observations about the game as Brooks led her out of the public space of the arena.

Aspen glanced up at her husband. "New adventure?"

"Yeah, I thought we might go to somewhere new. Maybe the Turks and Caicos Islands? Are you up for that?"

Heedless of the sweat, she looped her arms around his shoulders. "With you, always."

CHOOSE YOUR NEXT ROMANCE

GROWN-UP summer camp shenanigans aren't over yet! There's one more book in the Summer Fling Trilogy! *The Summer Camp Swap* is an expansion of one of my Meet Cute Romance novelettes—*Once Upon a Campfire.* I was never happy with the shorter version of the story and took this as an opportunity to deepen the relationship between Sarah and Beckett. This twin-swap secret identity is a must read for fans of *The Parent Trap* and any other zany tale that involves twins pretending to be each other.

Preorder your copy of *The Summer Camp Swap* today! It releases July 26, 2024!

Keep turning the pages for a sneak peek.

SNEAK PEEK THE SUMMER CAMP SWAP

It was a terrible idea.

But that doesn't stop Sarah Meadows from saying yes to covering for her identical twin sister at staff orientation week at Camp Firefly Falls. It's just two weeks, then she'll be back to finishing the master's thesis she's been stalled out on. But when her sexy, ex-park ranger partner figures out her secret, she's got her work cut out convincing him not to turn her in.

Beckett Hayes knows he should report Sarah to the boss, but instead, he finds himself agreeing to train her. He can't resist an underdog, and there's just something about those big, doe eyes and all that sass. But when Sarah starts to matter more than he planned, the pressure's on. Can he convince her to take the road less traveled or will these two weeks have to be enough?

"I need you to impersonate me."

From the faded corduroy sofa in her tiny, studio apartment, Sarah Meadows rolled her eyes, though her sister on the other end of the phone couldn't see. "Did you forget to renew your driver's license again? Because it expired back in January."

"I wish it were something that simple," Taryn said. "I've got a serious problem."

Sarah tensed at the words. "What is it this time?" She tried to keep the judgment out of her voice. Really, she did. But it was hard. So much of her twin's adult life had been a train wreck, and it seemed Sarah was routinely the one called upon to pick up the pieces and deal with the fallout.

"Well, you know I was supposed to be done with this private tour guide gig day after tomorrow and flying back East in time to start the new job at Camp Firefly Falls on Saturday, right?"

"Yeah. You've got orientation starting this weekend."

"I'm not going to make it back in time."

Oh, not good. Not good at all. "Why? What happened? Did your flight get cancelled? Because it's not too late to reschedule."

"No. This job came in last night—a two-week-long trek for some Hollywood muckitymuck."

Sarah couldn't stop the exasperated sigh. "You are *not* blowing off the camp job for one last guide trip." Dear God, she'd thought her sister was past this kind of impulsivity.

"No, it's not like that. I told Danny I couldn't do it. But he's threatening not to give me my last month's pay if I don't stick around and do it."

"You haven't been paid in a *month?*"

"Room and board were covered, and I figured if I didn't have the money in hand, I couldn't blow it on anything stupid. Except now I risk not getting paid at all, and I need that money, Sarah."

That was putting things mildly. Three years before, Taryn's unfortunate taste in men had resulted in a short relationship with one Jax Howorth—not his real name—who'd taken every dime of Taryn's money, trashed her credit, and left her under a mountain of debt. She'd been slowly, painstakingly climbing out of that hole ever since.

Sarah sighed. "How much are we talking?"

Her sister named a figure that had Sarah's mouth dropping open.

"You're getting paid that much as a guide?" Maybe she'd chosen the wrong career. Not that anybody became a grad student to make money. The hope was that you'd make enough when you finished the degree that you'd pay off whatever student loans you'd acquired before retirement.

"Rich people will pay for all kinds of things. And this producer guy, or whoever, is willing to give me a five *thousand* dollar bonus to stick around."

That had all of Sarah's alarm bells ringing. "Are you sure he doesn't expect you to do something more than be a trail guide?"

"Positive. He's flamingly gay."

Well, that was something, at least. "So, what exactly are you asking?"

"I want you to go to Camp Firefly Falls and be me for orientation. I'll be done with this job, get paid, and be back in time for the certification test. Nobody will be any the wiser."

Sarah shoved to her feet and began to pace. Ten steps to the kitchen. Fifteen to the window overlooking the busy Brooklyn street. Five to her bedroom door, then start again. "Taryn, this isn't like fooling our high school teachers. This is a job! One that you're qualified for, and I'm not. And what about you actually learning the stuff you're being certified *for?*"

"I've learned the handbook backwards and forwards, and there's nothing a camp in the Berkshires can throw at me that's harder than what I've been doing in Wyoming."

"That may be, but *I'm* not trained for any of this! How do you expect anybody to believe that I'm you?"

"It's not that complicated, sis. You're in good shape. You're a trained lifeguard, a runner. And God knows, you haven't met a subject you can't study up on and pass a test for. You just have to spend a couple weeks learning their policies and procedures, helping get camp set up, readying cabins, and that kind of thing. Easy peasy."

"Yeah, that's what you said when you convinced me to fill in at cheerleading practice so you could meet up with that college guy. 'Kick high, shake your thing, you'll be fine,' you said, 'they'll never know the difference.' Only you failed to mention the pyramid, and trust me, when it all came down, everyone knew the difference." Sarah felt a twinge in her back at the memory.

The noise at the other end of the line sounded

suspiciously like a stifled snort of laughter. Taryn cleared her throat. "In my defense, I didn't think they would try the pyramid. Man they were pissed." This was always the way. Her twin saw the humor in everything and never seemed to manage to take anything seriously.

"Not making your case here, Sis."

"But pissed at me, they were pissed at me. And no human pyramid at camp, no polyester, and no shaking your thing unless you're so inclined. But preferably not, because, you know, I have to work with these people."

"I'm smarter than I was at seventeen. Too smart to let you drag me into this. Besides, I do have a life. Responsibilities. I can't just pick up and go play you for two weeks."

"Oh, come on. Like you can't take a couple weeks off from your thesis?"

Sarah fought not to grind her teeth. "I can't, actually. I'm on a very strict schedule in order to finish in time to defend in August and start the doctoral program in the fall." She'd scrimped and saved in order to take the summer off from any assistantships so she could just write and be done with the thing. She wasn't about to waste that time.

"But just imagine how much clearer your head

will be after getting out of the city. You said yourself, you have a hard time writing there. You've been dying to get out of New York. This is your chance to recharge a little. And it's beautiful. You could take your camera, finally have some of the nature you actually *like* shooting pictures of."

A car horn blared from the street below and somebody shouted an inventive curse in... was that Portuguese?

A muscle by Sarah's eye began to twitch. "By working for you."

"Pleeeeeeease," Taryn wheedled. "Think about it, Sarah! Five *thousand*. It's enough to put a serious dent in the stupid debt. Enough I might be able to pay the last of it off by the end of the summer, so I can finally have a clean slate."

A clean slate. That had been Taryn's Holy Grail since Jax had walked out of her life. He'd been her wakeup call, the last in a long line of poor decisions. The school of hard knocks had taught her what no one else could, and she was finally ready to grow up. If she finally could get free of the mess Jax had created, she'd be able to do that. And Sarah would be able to stop worrying about her and focus on her own work.

Maybe.

But could she really afford two whole weeks away?

The living room wall rattled as something solid slammed against it from the apartment next door. A moan and the rhythmic thumping that followed told her it was the newlyweds going at it again, instead of a nice, helpful home invasion that would put an end to the ear-splitting noise violations they engaged in multiple times a day. The eye-twitch ramped up to a full on headache. Not only were they supremely distracting, but their enthusiastic amour only served to highlight exactly how long it had been since there'd been a man in her life.

Not that she was looking.

Sarah pinched the bridge of her nose. "You *swear* this is something I can pull off?"

"Absolutely!" Taryn assured her.

She was probably going to regret this. But maybe her twin was right and getting back to nature would help break the writer's block that had been plaguing her for months. At the very least, maybe she'd get some shots to replace the artwork on her walls.

"Okay. Against my better judgment, I'm in. Tell me what I need to do."

"GOOD MORNING, STAFFERS!"

From one of the picnic tables set up down by Lake Waawaatesi, Beckett Hayes watched his new boss, Heather Tully, address the assembled crowd. Oh yeah. His buddy, Michael, had done well when he'd married her. The cheerful blonde looked absolutely in her element. And why shouldn't she? Camp Firefly Falls—summer camp resort for grown-ups—was her brain child, and it had been a roaring success.

"It's going to be a super busy couple of weeks as we finish prepping for our first session of the summer—Singles Week—so we'll be throwing you all into the deep end with that one."

"Deep end is right," the guy next to him whispered. "I was here for that last year. It's like policing a damned orgy."

"Great," Beckett drawled. He'd dealt with some of that in his last job as national park ranger. Herding drunk, horny people was never fun. It almost always ended in insults and often with beer or other questionable liquids spilled on his uniform.

"Now, some of you will be here all summer and

some will be in and out, depending on the specifics of the session, but everybody has to pass their camp certification by the end of next week to keep our insurance company happy. That said, we want all of you to have fun yourselves. Here at Camp Firefly Falls, we work hard and play hard. The work begins bright and early at eight every morning. You can pick up your daily assignments at breakfast. We wrap in time for dinner at six, with evening activities planned so you can get to know your fellow staff members."

The collective staff cheered.

"This afternoon, we're getting started with a swim test."

"Are you serious?" someone called from down front.

"Camp rules. Everybody has to tread water for two minutes, then swim out to the raft and back. Anybody who does not pass will *not* be on any water activities for the summer. Anybody who's not already suited up, go change. We get rolling in fifteen minutes!"

Beckett held himself back from the minor stampede toward the staff cabins to change clothes. He was already set with board shorts and a T-shirt. While waiting, he scanned the remaining faces, noting the animated conversations and laughter. A lot of these people were returning staff, and a fair chunk had been campers here before the Tullys bought it and turned it into a resort, back when Camp Firefly Falls had been a regular sleep-away camp for kids.

Beckett hadn't been one of them.

Michael wandered over and plunked down on the other side of the table. "Settling in okay?"

"Getting there."

"Cabin working out for you?"

Beckett laughed. "It's like a damned penthouse suite compared to some of the places I lived with the park service. Listen, I want to thank you again for giving me a job this summer. After the—" He cut himself off, not wanting to get into the mess of his former position. "Well, my prospects weren't great. This is really saving my ass." The summer's work would buy him time to figure out his next move.

"Hey, it's our gain and my pleasure. They were wrong for firing you."

Beckett jerked his shoulders. "Yeah, well, I was far from the only one." His position and those of many other had been cut along with funding for so many of the national park programs. Things were improving some with the new administration, but those kinds of reversals took time to actually trickle down.

They both looked out over Lake Waawaatesi, glistening in the afternoon sun. It was gorgeous, soothing, and a far cry from the Ivy League campus where they'd met.

"Never would have thought we'd end up here when we were busting our humps for our MBAs," Beckett observed.

"Maybe not me, but you walked away from the crazy a lot sooner than I did."

In his last year of grad school, Beckett had walked out. Of the classroom. Of the MBA program. Away from Dartmouth. He'd never looked back. "Wasn't gonna make me happy."

"I wish I'd figured the same out sooner. That whole corporate culture nearly cost me my wife."

"But it didn't," Beckett observed. "This place brought you two back together."

Michael sighed in obvious contentment. "Seems fitting since we were camp sweethearts as kids."

He tipped back his water. "You're a lucky bastard."

"Yes, yes I am. And hey, who knows? Maybe you'll meet your match this summer."

Beckett cocked an eyebrow at his friend.

"Come on, now. I expect that kind of crap from Heather. Not from you."

Michael just grinned. "We've got a bulletin board up in Pinecone Lodge with pictures of all the couples who've gotten together here. It's filling up."

"You, sir, are full of shit."

Laughing, Michael shoved back from the table. "Just don't let Heather hear you say that. She'll try to matchmake you."

"I do not need the complication of a woman in my life." His own prospects were so uncertain at the moment, why would any woman even consider getting involved with him? He'd had few enough girlfriends over the years. None of them had been able to tolerate the semi-itinerant lifestyle of a park ranger. When his transfer to Yosemite had come up, his girlfriend at the time hadn't wanted to move with him, and he hadn't cared enough to want to stay. Since then, Beckett hadn't bothered with anything more than casual. If that had gotten old some time ago, well, such was life right now. He had other things to figure out.

"They're the only complication that's worth it." Michael's voice pulled Beckett back to the present.

"Spoken like the happily married man you are.

And on that saccharine note, I believe I'll take my position at the starting line." He stripped off his T-shirt and toed off his Chacos, leaving them in a neat pile on the picnic table as he went to join the thickening crowd on the dock.

He found himself next to a long, lean woman bent in a forward fold. He made a valiant effort not to stare at her ass in the snug, racer-back swimsuit and ended up admiring her gorgeously toned legs instead.

"See something you like?" The wry tone had him yanking his eyes away like a teenage boy caught peeping in the girls' locker room.

Busted.

"Sorry," Beckett muttered, gaze now firmly on the raft anchored out in the center of the lake. "You just look—" Was there any way to finish that sentence that didn't make him come off like a perv? "—like you know what you're doing."

"I should. I've been swimming competitively practically since birth." She straightened. "I'm Taryn."

He interpreted the proffered hand as a sign of forgiveness and turned to take it. His own name died on his tongue as he found himself faced with the biggest doe eyes he'd ever seen.

Well hello, Bambi.

"Hi."

A corner of Taryn's mouth quirked as she gave his hand a perfunctory shake. "May the best swimmer win."

"Win wha—"

The scream of an air horn signaled the start of the test. Taryn dove for the water, as did everyone around Beckett before he could get his brain in gear. She'd already surfaced by the time he dove in. The chill lake water was a shock to his system, clearing the haze of lust from his brain.

"Two minutes!" Heather shouted. "Starting... now!"

His feet and arms automatically began to tread, keeping him afloat. A few feet away, Taryn was already facing the raft, her dark blonde hair slicked back like a seal.

"In a hurry?" he asked.

She glanced over her shoulder one corner of her mouth quirked. "Eye on the target."

"You know this isn't a contest, right?"

Her lips bowed into a full-on grin that sucker punched him more than the icy lake. "Everything's a competition."

Beckett had done everything in his power to get away from competition in his life. But something about that smile pulled at him and invited him to join in the fun. He had a feeling competition with Taryn would be anything but the senseless, boring grind he'd walked away from. So he readied muscles honed as a boy in the surf off Myrtle Beach, and when Heather blew the air horn again, he went for it.

He made it to the head of the pack in four strokes, but Taryn was faster. Her freestyle was a thing of beauty, slicing cleanly through the water as if she'd been born to it. Beckett dug deep, pulling his focus back to his own form. Half a dozen strokes and he'd closed the gap to two lengths. Ahead, Taryn slapped the raft and dove, popping back up and heading toward shore. Beckett tagged the raft himself and switched to butterfly for the return leg. He caught up with her at the halfway point. Seeing what he was about, she shifted smoothly into a butterfly stroke herself, and they both raced for the finish line.

Taryn beat him by two strokes. Beckett could hear her crow of victory as she slapped the dock.

"You are a freaking mermaid," he gasped.

She slicked her hair back and beamed. "Yes, I am. God, that felt good!"

A shadow fell over the two of them. Michael. "You realize we have no prizes, right?"

"Maybe you should," Beckett suggested. "Because that was damned impressive."

"Maybe we'll just move things around so she's on lifeguard duty instead of paired up with you for rock climbing."

"Looks like tomorrow we get to go to *my* playground." Beckett grinned, turning to the mermaid. Something had wiped the smile clear off her face. In fact, she looked a little sick. What was that about?

He hauled himself out of the water and reached down to offer a hand to Taryn. "You okay?"

Eschewing his hand, she hoisted herself cleanly up, the water sluicing off that long, lean body. "I'm fine." She reached for a towel, hastily wrapping it around herself before muttering, "See you tomorrow."

Then she was gone and Beckett was left wondering what the hell he'd done wrong.

Michael smirked at him. "What was that you said about not needing the complication of a woman?"

"Still true. But I'm breathing, so I can appreciate the distraction of one when she appears."

His buddy just laughed. "I call that denial, but whatever helps you sleep at night, pal."

. . .

PREORDER your copy of *The Summer Camp Swap* today!

OTHER BOOKS BY KAIT NOLAN

A complete and up-to-date list of all my books can be found at https://kaitnolan.com.

KILTED HEARTS
SMALL TOWN CONTEMPORARY SCOTTISH ROMANCE

- *Jilting The Kilt* (prequel)
- *Cowboy in a Kilt* (Raleigh and Kyla)
- *Grump in a Kilt* (Malcolm and Charlotte)
- *Playboy in a Kilt* (Connor and Sophie)
- *Protector in a Kilt* (Ewan and Isobel)
- *Single Dad in a Kilt* (Hamish and Afton)
- *Kilty Pleasures* (Jason and Skye)

BAD BOY BAKERS
SMALL TOWN MILITARY ROMANCE

- *Rescued By a Bad Boy* (Brax and Mia prequel)
- *Mixed Up With a Marine* (Brax and Mia)
- *Wrapped Up with a Ranger* (Holt and Cayla)
- *Stirred Up by a SEAL* (Jonah and Rachel)
- *Hung Up on the Hacker* (Cash and Hadley)
- *Caught Up with the Captain* (Grey and Rebecca)

RESCUE MY HEART SERIES
SMALL TOWN MILITARY ROMANCE

- *Someone Like You* (Ivy and Harrison)
- *What I Like About You* (Laurel and Sebastian)
- *Bad Case of Loving You* (Paisley and Ty prequel) Included in *Made For Loving You* (Paisley and Ty)

THE MISFIT INN SERIES
SMALL TOWN FAMILY ROMANCE

- *When You Got A Good Thing* (Kennedy and Xander)
- *Til There Was You* (Misty and Denver)
- *Those Sweet Words* (Pru and Flynn)
- *Stay A Little Longer* (Athena and Logan)
- *Bring It On Home* (Maggie and Porter)
- *Come Away with Me* (Moses and Zuri)

MEN OF THE MISFIT INN
SMALL TOWN SOUTHERN ROMANCE

- *Let It Be Me* (Emerson and Caleb)
- *Our Kind of Love* (Abbey and Kyle)
- *Don't You Wanna Stay* (Deanna and Wyatt)
- *Until We Meet Again* (Samantha and Griffin prequel)
- *Come A Little Closer* (Samantha and Griffin)
- *Just Wanted You To Know* (Livia and Declan)
- *A Love Like You* (Juliette and Mick)

SUMMER FLING TRILOGY
CONTEMPORARY ROMANCE

- *Second Chance Summer* (Audrey and Hudson)
- *Summer Camp Secret* (Aspen and Brooks)
- *The Summer Camp Swap* (Sarah and Beckett)

WISHFUL ROMANCE SERIES
SMALL TOWN SOUTHERN ROMANCE

- *Once Upon A Coffee* (Avery and Dillon)
- *To Get Me To You* (Cam and Norah)
- *Know Me Well* (Liam and Riley)
- *Be Careful, It's My Heart* (Brody and Tyler)
- *Just For This Moment* (Myles and Piper)
- *Wish I Might* (Reed and Cecily)
- *Turn My World Around* (Tucker and Corinne)
- *Dance Me A Dream* (Jace and Tara)
- *See You Again* (Trey and Sandy)
- *The Christmas Fountain* (Chad and Mary Alice)
- *You Were Meant For Me* (Mitch and Tess)
- *A Lot Like Christmas* (Ryan and Hannah)
- *Dancing Away With My Heart* (Zach and Lexi)

WISHING FOR A HERO SERIES (A WISHFUL SPINOFF SERIES)
SMALL TOWN ROMANTIC SUSPENSE

- *Make You Feel My Love* (Judd and Autumn)
- *Watch Over Me* (Nash and Rowan)
- *Can't Take My Eyes Off You* (Ethan and Miranda)
- *Burn For You* (Sean and Delaney)

MEET CUTE ROMANCE
SMALL TOWN SHORT ROMANCE

- *Once Upon A Snow Day*
- *Once Upon A New Year's Eve*
- *Once Upon An Heirloom*
- *Once Upon A Coffee*
- *Once Upon A Campfire*
- *Once Upon A Rescue*

ABOUT KAIT

Kait is a Mississippi native, who often swears like a sailor, calls everyone sugar, honey, or darlin', and can wield a bless your heart like a saber or a Snuggie, depending on requirements.

You can find more information on this *USA Today* best selling and RITA ® Award-winning author and her books on her website http://kait nolan.com.

Do you need more small town sass and spark? Sign up for <u>her newsletter</u> to hear about new re-leases, book deals, and exclusive content!